"You have to trust me."

Kylie looked away, unable to meet the hurt that she knew would be in his eyes.

Mark gave her hand a gentle squeeze. "I get it. Half the time I don't even trust myself. I'll talk to Matthew and Parker. I'm sure Junie would rather stay with them. I'll stay with Dad. Is there anything that needs to be done at your place? Pets to feed?"

She rolled over to face him, shivering beneath the white hospital blanket.

He knew she'd never had pets and still didn't. Her mom had brought home every stray she'd found, including people. The trailer she'd grown up in had always been overrun with mangy dogs and flea-bitten cats, as well as "friends" of her mother.

"No pets. And thank you for understanding."

"Trust me. With this, you can trust me." He sounded so sincere. "I'll be here as long as the two of you need me."

Trust him. What choice did she have?

Brenda Minton lives in the Ozarks with her husband, children, cats, dogs and strays. She is a pastor's wife, Sunday-school teacher, coffee addict and is sleep-deprived. Not in that order. Her dream to be an author for Harlequin started somewhere in the pages of a romance novel about a young American woman stranded in a Spanish castle. Her dreams came true, and twenty-plus books later, she is an author hoping to inspire young girls to dream.

Books by Brenda Minton

Love Inspired

Sunset Ridge

Reunited by the Baby
A Valentine's Day Return

Her Small Town Secret
Her Christmas Dilemma
Earning Her Trust

Mercy Ranch

Reunited with the Rancher
The Rancher's Christmas Match
Her Oklahoma Rancher
The Rancher's Holiday Hope
The Prodigal Cowboy
The Rancher's Holiday Arrangement

Visit the Author Profile page at LoveInspired.com for more titles.

A Valentine's Day Return

Brenda Minton

LOVE INSPIRED
INSPIRATIONAL ROMANCE

LOVE INSPIRED®

INSPIRATIONAL ROMANCE

Recycling programs for this product may not exist in your area.

ISBN-13: 978-1-335-59717-5

A Valentine's Day Return

Copyright © 2024 by Brenda Minton

All rights reserved. No part of this book may be used or reproduced in any manner whatsoever without written permission except in the case of brief quotations embodied in critical articles and reviews.

This is a work of fiction. Names, characters, places and incidents are either the product of the author's imagination or are used fictitiously. Any resemblance to actual persons, living or dead, businesses, companies, events or locales is entirely coincidental.

For questions and comments about the quality of this book, please contact us at CustomerService@Harlequin.com.

Love Inspired
22 Adelaide St. West, 41st Floor
Toronto, Ontario M5H 4E3, Canada
www.LoveInspired.com

Printed in U.S.A.

Husbands, love your wives, even as Christ also loved the church, and gave himself for it.
—*Ephesians* 5:25

This book is dedicated to Susan Gibson Snodgrass,
because she shared her beautiful words
about our words. She encouraged and she shone
her light so brightly in her faith and her marriage.
To Tom Snodgrass, who loved her deeply.
Romance written on our pages
pales in comparison to what the two of you shared.

Chapter One

The town of Sunset Ridge, Oklahoma, had changed a lot since Mark Rivers left. He'd been eighteen the day he hit the road in an old pickup truck a lot like the one he drove today. A truck that smelled of oil and the farm, with cloth-and-vinyl seats and a faded red dash and more faded fake-wood trim. These days, he could afford better, but he'd bought this truck when his plane landed in Tulsa. A truck that took him back to his roots.

He pulled around the square, past Chuck's Café, past the thrift store and the antique store, then found a parking space a short distance from Kylie's Coffee Shop and Bakery. It was late on Sunday night. They weren't at home. Church had let out an hour earlier. He couldn't think of anywhere else they might be. His guess had been correct. The lights to the coffee shop were on.

He cut the engine, then he just sat there letting the cold January air seep in, not getting out, not confronting his past or his mistakes. Yeah, he guessed it might be true that he was a coward, but going in there wouldn't be easy. He'd hurt his wife, scratch that, his ex-wife, and his daughter, and he doubted either of them were ready to forgive.

He didn't blame them. There were times he didn't know if he could forgive himself.

From inside the truck, he watched as his…as Kylie hung cut-out hearts and white twinkling lights in the windows of her little shop with its green awning and bistro-style furniture. Through the big glass window, he saw her smile at their daughter, saw the light shimmer off her hair. She'd dyed it a silvery gray color. He liked it, even though he also loved her natural, dark hair color. Junie, now six, held the ends of the lights and said something that made them both laugh.

Junie. From birth, she'd had those dark curls and big eyes that made her daddy want to spoil her rotten and never let her cry. Too bad he'd been the cause of her tears.

Man, they were beautiful, his wife and daughter. They were the two biggest blessings in his life. He'd overlooked their value and picked the things that had landed him in the gutter.

He'd never get them back, he knew that. He didn't want them back, not if there was any chance that he'd hurt them again. No, they were better off without him.

They didn't need him. Watching them through the window, that seemed obvious. They were happy in this life they'd built for themselves. They were laughing and smiling, two things they hadn't done when they'd been with him. As he watched, Kylie twirled their daughter in lights, and then she took a quick picture of the two of them together.

They might not need him in their lives, but they did need for him to be a better person. They needed to be able to depend on him.

That started now.

He had to go in and make things right. He guessed

seeing him clean and sober would be almost as surprising as the last time they'd seen him.

That hadn't been one of his finer moments. What he could remember of it. One thing he did remember, the look on Junie's face when he stumbled through the doors of the church, crashing into his brother's wedding. At the memory, his hands clenched on the steering wheel, seeing it as clearly as if it had just happened. Junie's expression had been branded into his memory.

A man had to get to a place of complete brokenness in order to get help. That had been his moment. He'd spent three months in rehab getting clean. He'd spent the past nine months out, living a sober life. All because of Junie and that day. He wanted to never see that look on her face, ever again.

He had to shed the persona of country musician Marcus Rivers, and he had to walk through the door of Kylie's shop a humbled man, seeking to make things right.

Casually, as if his heart didn't plan to beat its way out of his chest, he exited the old truck. He pushed the door closed, having already realized it didn't much like latching. The air was crisp, but not cold. It was the middle of January, and winter had settled over the countryside, leaving the grass brown and trees bare. The lights and tinsel of Christmas were gone.

He faced Kylie's little shop, the one he'd helped her purchase. She'd supported his dreams of becoming a country singer, so it made sense that he'd helped her gain her dream of having a coffee shop and bakery.

As he approached the door, his hands began to sweat, and he felt a little queasy. He'd never been as confident as he let the world think. His swagger and courage had come from the bottle, and now he had to find a new brand of strength. He'd found strength in renewing his faith. He guessed that eventually he'd even find a little faith in his own abilities.

From her perch on the ladder, she noticed him. It didn't take him by surprise, the way her dark eyes widened, the way she went pale. The shock turned to loathing in the space of a heartbeat. *Loathing*, that had to be the only word that fit the expression on Kylie's face.

Make amends, his sponsor had insisted. To move forward, this step must happen. It had to be more than an apology. It had to be about making things right. Not only for his wife and daughter, but for himself. He drew in a breath and prayed for more strength.

He entered the shop, the jingly-jangly bells ringing a cheerful greeting. Kylie stepped down from the ladder. Junie moved to her mother's side, her startled gaze shifting from one parent to the other. He'd thought of numerous greetings, but in the moment, he couldn't think of a single thing to say, or anything that made sense.

"Honey, I'm home." Not the greeting he'd practiced.

And yet he'd done it anyway. As the words slipped out, he closed his eyes and groaned.

"You still have a way with words," Kylie said. "What are you doing here, Mark?"

"I'm taking a little break." More than a break. "I came home to spend time with my dad." Those were also not the words he'd planned, because he hadn't planned on spending time with Buck at the ranch his brother Matthew had decided to bring back to life.

Dealing with Buck might be on the to-do list, but Kylie and Junie came first. He should tell her that, or something along those lines.

"Oh, I see." She pulled Junie a little closer, a gesture

that hurt more than anything she might have said. "We were just closing up for the day."

He remained frozen to the cheery sunflower welcome mat, not daring to go any farther. He smiled down at his daughter. She was the best of the two of them. She had Kylie's dark eyes; her curls came from him, and that stubborn tip of her chin, well, it seemed a perfect imitation of her mother's at that moment.

In all the times he'd played this reunion through, he guessed he hadn't really pictured how they'd react to his visit. He'd thought about what he'd say and how he'd say it, but he hadn't thought about them. Again, he'd been thinking of himself.

That had to stop. This wasn't for him, it was for Kylie and Junie.

Kylie cleared her throat, and he shifted his attention to her. She'd lost weight. Because of him? It would make sense.

"I should have called," he said as he glanced down at the sparkly gift bag he'd carried in.

"Probably," Kylie said. "But you're here, so you might as well say what you've come to say."

He cleared his throat. "I'm sorry."

"Mark, please just…" she waved her hand, a gesture that told him to carry on. Junie had moved a little in his direction, her eyes wide with curiosity. It had been too long, and he'd not known the impact of the long months of separation until that moment.

"Hey, June Bug," he greeted as he went down on one knee to put himself at eye level with his daughter. No one wanted to be towered over, especially if the situation already felt dire. "I brought you a gift from Nashville."

Little teeth bit down on her bottom lip, unsure. He

held out the bag with its tissue paper and multicolored ribbons. After a few long seconds, she took it, glancing up at Kylie to make sure she had permission. Curiosity overcame her, and she peeked inside. A smile grew as she reached into the bag and pulled out a music box. It was an intricate doodad that he'd picked up at a shop on Music Row. Probably the wrong gift for a little girl, but he'd thought it pretty when he spotted it inside the glass case at the store. She could shake it like a snow globe and cause tiny flakes to fall upon the Grand Ole Opry, or she could wind it up and listen to Loretta Lynn singing "Wildwood Flower."

On second thought, he regretted the gift and the song. A song of a love that had been misused and left by a wandering man who broke a woman's heart. The worst possible song—he'd just always loved the tune. He briefly closed his eyes.

"Nice," Kylie whispered, and he looked up just in time to see her swipe away a tear.

"I…" What did he say? "I'm sorry."

"For the music box?" Junie asked in a quiet voice that interrupted their conversation and reminded them of her presence.

Mark inhaled and prayed God would give him the right words for the situation. A situation of his own making.

"No," he started, looking from his daughter to her mother. "I'm sorry for so much—I don't know where to start. I should have written down all the reasons I owe you an apology and need your forgiveness."

"That would be a long list," Kylie said, her tone dry.

He studied her face, really studied it. The hint of amusement in her dark eyes reminded him of their early days. They'd been childhood friends and then teens falling in love. At seventeen, she'd joined him in Nashville, wanting the adventure and believing in his ability to succeed. He had found success, and then he'd ruined everything, including them.

Even at thirty-one, he still saw hints of the girl he'd known. She was tall, only inches shorter than him. She'd grown slimmer since leaving him. Junie, on the other hand, with her curls and rounded cheeks, seemed to be thriving.

"It would be a long list," he agreed. "I'm not sure where to start."

"Mommy isn't feeling well—we should go home now." Junie spoke, the music box still clutched in her tiny hands.

"I'm fine," Kylie inserted with a firm voice. "We aren't going home just yet. I need to have these decorations up by morning. With Christmas over, we're moving on to Valentine's Day."

"I can help," Mark offered.

"No, we can do it." Junie again, her rosebud lips pursed in a perfect imitation of her mother. He smiled at her, wishing he had been a better father. Praying he could be a father again and make up for the times he'd failed her, for the years he'd lost.

"Junie," Kylie warned. "Always be respectful."

Junie opened her mouth as if to add something, but a quick look at her mother stopped the words.

"Excuse me," Kylie said as she pushed her hand to her mouth and hurried from the room.

That left Mark with his daughter.

"Junie, I'm really very sorry for hurting you and upsetting you. I haven't been the best dad." He paused at the expression on her little face. He didn't have a clue how he should talk to his daughter. "I've not been a dad at all. I hope to make that up to you."

She gave him a quick look, her head tilted to the side and her expression far too wise. After a few seconds, she nodded. "It's okay, Mark. I forgive you."

"Do you?" he asked, trying not to be hurt by the use of his first name.

"Yes, I do. We learned about forgiving in Sunday school. There's a verse I can't remember, but it's important to forgive."

"I'll look those verses up," he promised her. He glanced toward the door to the back of the shop. "Do you think we should check on her?"

Junie shook her head. "She'll be back. She's been sick all week, but she won't listen to Aunt Parker. Aunt Parker said she needs to go in and get checked. Aunt Parker is a nurse. You ruined her wedding."

He whistled soft and low at that. "Yeah, I guess I owe her an apology, too."

"She's the one who taught me about forgiving. If you ask, she'll forgive you." She leaned in close, as if telling him a secret. "Some wounds take more time to heal."

"Aunt Parker?" he whispered back.

Junie nodded.

Kylie still hadn't returned. He was caught between the urge to help and to mind his own business. She'd left him four years ago and made it clear he could see his daughter, but would no longer be welcome in her life.

"Should we go ahead and finish hanging these lights?" he asked Junie.

"I don't know," she frowned as she looked from him to the string of lights. "Maybe."

"I'll get on the ladder. You can hand them up."

She nodded, accepting the plan. He shouldn't have

felt elated over the tiny hint of acceptance, but he did. Elated on one hand, worried on the other. Kylie had yet to return.

Kylie leaned against the wall, trembling, her legs weak. It felt as if a hot knife sliced through her abdomen, and the pain, unlike the other times, didn't seem to be abating. As she tried to take a step, the pain nearly brought her to her knees.

Of all the times for Mark to show up, why now? She didn't want him here to witness her illness. She didn't want to be doubled over in pain, feeling vulnerable, while he looked better than ever and smelled like an expensive trip to a Caribbean island.

He'd broken her heart. He'd used up all of her loyalty, in the process destroying every ounce of love she'd had for him. She could forgive him. That didn't mean she wanted him in her life or her shop.

They shared a daughter. She had to remind herself that he had a right to see Junie, to be in her life. Junie wanted to see her father. Didn't every little girl? As a child who'd grown up with a single mother, Kylie knew the pain of missing out on a father.

It had been so much simpler with him in Tennessee and the two of them in Oklahoma. Absence hadn't made the heart grow fonder—it had just helped hers to heal.

Taking a few deep breaths, she found the strength to walk out of the bathroom. She would make this quick. She'd let him say whatever he needed to say, and then she'd go home to a cup of tea and her warmest robe.

As she entered the dining room, she managed to remain upright. The last thing she wanted was to collapse on the floor in a puddle of tears and sickness. *Bright smile*, she urged herself. *Pretend everything is fine.* She looked up to a scene that could have been on the front of a greeting card.

Junie stood by the window, the twinkling lights wrapped around her body. Kylie's gaze traveled up. Mark stood on the ladder, his jeans low on his hips, his faded red sweatshirt snug across his shoulders. His hair, always curly, was more controlled these days. He hadn't shaved in a few days, or perhaps that was his new style, scruffy. She disliked that she noticed how cute he was or the way his silver-gray eyes sought approval when he caught her watching.

"Ky, you okay?" he asked, using the nickname he'd given her the year she'd turned twelve. They'd been riding bikes around town and then they'd headed to the creek to wade in the icy cold water.

"I'm good," she tried to reassure him and their daughter. She reached for the counter, doing her best to stay upright.

"Mommy?" Junie clearly didn't believe she was okay.

"I'm fine," Kylie repeated, to them and to herself. "I just need to go home and rest."

Mark hopped down from the ladder and moved to her side. Gently, he felt her forehead, as if temperature checking came naturally to him. Then he leaned and pressed his lips to her brow, the way she often did to Junie. "You're burning up."

"I'm not," she told him. "I'm good. It's just a virus."

"Aunt Parker says it's not a virus. She said you should go to the doctor." Junie said it with her chin up, a fight to be strong as tears filled her eyes.

"I promise you, I'm okay. I'm going to go home and rest. By tomorrow, I'll be good as new." She wiped a tear from Junie's cheek.

The last thing she wanted was to cause her daughter to worry. Her goal in life had been to give Junie a childhood without fear. A childhood. Period.

Kylie's own mother had stolen her childhood. Mindy Waters, Kylie's mom, had loved drugs more than she'd loved her own daughter. She'd loved drugs more than life. Raised by an addict, married to an addict. Kylie shook her head, freeing herself from the past and the pain of her childhood and the pain of watching Mark become a person she'd never expected him to be.

He gave her a long look and then slowly shook his head. "Don't." He leaned in and whispered the word close to her ear. "Don't go there."

He knew her too well.

"Junie, I'm fine. I promise." Kylie smiled down at her daughter as she put space between herself and Mark. "Remember, faith, not fear."

Junie sniffled, but she nodded. "Faith, not fear."

"Let me drive the two of you home," Mark offered.

She started to object, but it didn't seem to be the right time for obstinance. If she were being honest, she didn't know if she could drive herself. "I'd appreciate the ride."

A few minutes and he had the lights off, had reset her thermostat and had grabbed her purse from under the counter. Junie followed him, giving him instructions on each thing he needed to do. Kylie couldn't help but smile as she watched the two of them.

As much as she didn't want Mark in her life, he needed to be in his daughter's life.

He finished all the details of closing up and returned to the table where he'd insisted she take a seat.

"Ready to go?" He reached for her hand and drew her to her feet.

"More than ready," she admitted. The pain had grown sharper, and she nearly doubled over as she stood.

"Maybe we should bypass the house and go to the emergency room?" he suggested, still holding her hand.

"Please just take us home."

He locked the door behind them and helped her to the faded red-and-white truck parked next to her Jeep. When he opened the door, she stepped back, overwhelmed by "old car" smell. She couldn't imagine this scent ever being used in a diffuser. It was a combination of age, motor oil and farm.

"I don't think I can get in there."

"It isn't that bad," he defended.

"The smell." She put a hand to her mouth. "I'm not trying to be rude. I just, my stomach."

He looked a little bit hurt, but when Junie wrinkled her nose, he leaned in to check for himself. "I guess it isn't springtime fresh in there."

"Could you drive my car? I think it would be easier to get in and definitely more comfortable."

He grinned, flashing a dimple that matched the one in Junie's right cheek. "I suppose we'll just leave 'old red' here for now. Hopefully no one takes her."

"I think she's safe," Kylie assured him.

He took the keys she offered and opened the passenger door of her Jeep. Junie climbed in the back and buckled into her booster seat as Kylie eased herself into the front. Mark leaned in to recline the seat, and then he gently eased the seatbelt around her waist. Her heart melted a little, and she had to close her eyes to distance herself from the emotions of having him so near, taking care of her. It felt reminiscent of the night he'd taken her to the hospital to have Junie.

Once upon a time, he'd been her handsome prince. He'd rescued her from a life of poverty and neglect. He'd put her on a pedestal. He'd even built her a castle.

He'd built it all, and then he'd broken her heart and left her empty. No, that wasn't true. He'd given her the best thing of all. He'd given her Junie. She would always have the best of him in their daughter.

A moment later, they were speeding through town in the direction of her new home. The house, formerly the Duncan place, had belonged to the lawyer in town. When she'd watched him with his family, she'd always wondered what it would be like to live in their two-story brick home with two parents and with children who always seemed happy and loved. His youngest daughter had even resembled Kylie, strengthening her childish fantasy.

A fantasy about a family that really had been hers, only they hadn't known she existed. She'd been the secret he kept with her mother.

Now she owned the house she'd never been allowed to enter. She'd thought to feel a sense of victory. Instead, she'd found peace and she'd let go of the anger she'd always felt for them.

Mark pulled into the drive, and she reached to push the button for the garage. "I'm sorry we left your truck. You can take my car for the night."

"I'm not crazy about leaving you alone."

"I'll be fine. If I need anything, I can call Parker."

He parked and took the keys from the ignition. "You can also call me."

She didn't have the strength to argue. Instead, she pushed her door open and tried to exit her car with some dignity, which didn't include losing more of her stomach contents on the floor of the garage. Unfortunately, she couldn't make it out of the car, not without his help.

"I can't do this," he said. "I can't take you inside and leave you. You need the emergency room."

The announcement made her want to cry. She would have cried if she'd had the energy. She couldn't even argue with him.

"I know," she said. "I kept thinking I would get better."

"Let me help you," he said with a tender smile. "I know that I've done a lot to hurt you, to hurt you both. Trust me to take care of you tonight."

She leaned back in the seat and closed her eyes. "I forgive you. You don't have to earn that forgiveness."

"I know that. Maybe there is a purpose in my presence here tonight. Maybe, just maybe, God planned for me to be at your shop because He knew you needed me there to help you."

"Maybe," she said, letting a few tears slide free.

"I'm going to call Parker," he told her. "Let's see what she says."

Again, she nodded. She had no fight left in her. She couldn't even turn her head to make sure Junie was okay. As if she knew, Junie reached up and placed her hand on Kylie's shoulder.

"It's okay, honey. I promise it'll be okay." Kylie patted Junie's hand.

She closed her eyes and listened as Mark gave Parker a brief rundown of her condition, and then he pushed the speaker icon, as if she needed to hear for herself.

"Mark, take her to the emergency room," Parker said. "We'll meet you there."

"It's just a virus," Kylie tried again.

Over the speaker, she heard Parker's sigh. "I think that argument has been lost."

"We'll see you there. And thank you." Mark ended the call. "Okay?"

She nodded, but words didn't come. She wanted to tell

him thank you. She wanted to say how much it meant that he was there for her. The words wouldn't come, not because she didn't want to say them, but because she physically couldn't get the words out. She felt like the worst kind of sissy as she drew her knees close and curled up in the seat.

A strong hand touched her arm. She raised her gaze to meet his and saw all of the strength of the man she'd always wanted him to be. She didn't want to need Mark, but his nearness felt familiar and comforting. His strength, the strength of the Mark she'd grown up with, helped her to relax, to take a breath. She wasn't alone. Junie wouldn't be alone.

As much as she didn't want to depend on him, for tonight, she needed to give up control and let him help. Not just for her sake, but also for Junie. It was much easier to let him help when she framed it that way. He was going to be there for Junie.

Chapter Two

Kylie shivered beneath the paper-thin blanket provided by the hospital. The nurse's aide had seemed so confident that the "just out of the warmer" blanket would have her "feeling better in no time." Whatever the woman thought about those blankets and their ability to "make things better," Kylie had to disagree. And she knew, without being told, that she was being disagreeable.

"When is the doctor going to be here?" she mumbled, wishing she could sneak a sip of water or ask for a cup of tea. She'd already been told that both were off-limits because they were positive they'd be doing an appendectomy as soon as it could be arranged.

"Soon," Mark assured her. One side of his mouth hitched up, deepening those dimples that were almost, but not quite, hidden by the ten o'clock shadow that covered his lean and perpetually tan cheeks.

"I want to go home."

Another grin. "I know. This feels a lot like when you were having Junie. The two of us together in a hospital. You complaining that you want to go home."

"Me in pain, and you finding it amusing."

His grin dissolved. "I'm not amused. I'm just trying to cheer you up and make this easier."

"I'm worried about Junie."

"I'll take care of her," he assured her.

She sighed, closing her eyes. "I'm sorry. I'm not a good patient."

"No, but you always manage to make a cloth sack look like designer clothing."

She reminded herself that he'd always been charming. He should have saved all of that charm for her. He should have...

A light rap on the door shook her from the "should have" thoughts. Those thoughts had nowhere to take her but into the dark past of their relationship, and she didn't want to go there, not now. Now was a time for faith and hope, not darkness and depression. The door opened and the doctor entered, glancing at her, at Mark and then, of course, at Mark again. She almost groaned at the obvious reaction.

Dr. Janson cleared his throat, professionalism back on track. "Mrs. Rivers, we are scheduling your surgery. We're going to try to get you back there as soon as possible."

"And then I can go home?" She managed to sound more hopeful than she felt.

He gave her a clearly sympathetic look. "I don't think you should plan on going home for a few days. We'll know more once we get in there, but what we're dealing with is a ruptured appendix and an infection."

He continued, and she tried to focus on what he described as a situation that could have been much worse if she hadn't come in when she did. She gave Mark a quick look and saw the downturn of his mouth and the way he drew in a breath.

"They'll be in here soon to prep you for surgery. I expect things to go well, but you have to understand that you're not going to be up and around in a matter of days."

Mark's hand had taken hers, and he gave a gentle squeeze. A reassuring, make-her-stronger squeeze. She didn't pull back, not then, maybe later when she didn't need him. They'd given her medicine for the pain; that explained the lowered defenses. Or at least that was what she told herself.

"I can't stay in the hospital. I have the coffee shop and Junie."

"You have yourself to take care of," Mark reminded her. "I'm here. I'll be here for you and for Junie."

"Parker and Matthew. I need to talk to them. Junie can stay with them. I know you didn't come here planning to stay and babysit. You probably have somewhere to be."

"She's my daughter, too, and it isn't babysitting." He brushed a hand through his hair and let out a breath.

"I have to know that she's going to be okay. She'll be worried. She's never been away from me."

"You have to trust me."

She looked away, unable to meet the hurt that she knew would be in his eyes.

He gave her hand a gentle squeeze. "I get it. Half the time, I don't even trust myself. I'll talk to Matthew and Parker. I'm sure Junie would rather stay with them. I'll stay with Dad. Is there anything that needs to be done at your place? Pets to feed?"

Kylie rolled over to face him, shivering beneath the white hospital blanket.

He knew she'd never had pets and still didn't. Her mom had brought home every stray she'd found, including people. The trailer she'd grown up in had always been overrun with mangy dogs and flea-bitten cats, as well as "friends" of her mother.

"No pets. And thank you for understanding."

"Trust me. With this, you can trust me." He sounded so sincere. "I'll be here as long as the two of you need me."

Trust him. What choice did she have? She closed her eyes on a wave of pain and worry. She didn't want to let the worry consume her. Didn't the Bible tell her that a person couldn't add a cubit to their stature by worrying? It wouldn't change her situation or the outcome to worry.

"Is Junie still in the waiting room?" she asked, an edge of panic creeping in. "I need to hug her."

"I'll get them," Mark spoke, his voice reverberating through her like the bass of a radio.

"Thank you."

The door snicked closed as he left, and for a few minutes, she had time alone, time to process the situation she found herself stuck in. She'd expected this illness to be just another virus that ran its course. She hadn't expected her ex-husband to waltz through the door of her coffee shop.

"Mommy?" Junie slipped into the room alone. Her dark eyes were luminous in her pale face. She stopped, taking in the room, the hospital bed, her mother.

"Come here, sweet girl. Let's cuddle." She held her arms open, and Junie hurried forward for the promised hug. "I'm going to be fine. They're going to do a surgery and take out my appendix, and in just a few days, I'll be good as new. Probably better."

"I don't want you to be gone."

"It's just a few days. I promise." Kylie pressed her

lips to her daughter's brow. "And you get to have a sleepover with Aunt Parker and Uncle Matthew. You probably even get to sleep in Faith's room."

Junie pulled back, her expression troubled. "Not Daddy?"

"He'll be around. He's going to stay a few days with your granddad."

"Will I get to see him?" Junie asked.

"I'm sure you will." Kylie's heart ached at the question. It had been so long since Mark had made an appearance. Now she knew why. He'd been getting sober. Junie was too young to process all of this.

The door opened. Junie sat up, watching to see who would join them. Kylie waited also, wondering if he'd stay, if he'd be there for Junie.

Parker and Matthew entered the room. No Mark.

"He's in the chapel," Matthew offered. "He needed a minute."

"Hmm," Kylie murmured. She couldn't say more, not in front of Junie. Matthew looked as if he wanted to say more. She wondered if he would defend his brother or give her words of warning as he'd done years ago, when she'd packed up her old Charger and told him she was going to Nashville to be with his brother.

Parker moved to her side. "Is there anything we can do, or get you?"

"I'd like water." Kylie smiled up at her friend.

"I wish I could." Parker winked at Junie. "I'm afraid no liquids."

"Where's Faith?" Kylie asked, hoping the conversation would keep her mind off the searing pain.

"She's with Melinda Carr. We'll pick her up on our way home."

Melinda, the church nursery worker and also a trusted babysitter for Faith and many other children in town.

"I'm so sorry you had to leave her and come out on a night like this. It's so cold."

Parker put a hand to Kylie's brow. "And you have a fever. Relax, we know that Faith is fine, and you're important to us. We want you well. It's good that Mark showed up when he did."

"Yes." She couldn't deny that fact. If he hadn't shown up, she would have gone home, the way she'd been going home for days, still sick and still believing she'd be better by morning.

After all these years, Mark was still coming to her rescue.

He'd been her hero, until he hadn't. She had no one to blame for that but herself. She'd looked to him to save her, to protect her from all harm. Unfortunately, he hadn't been able to save himself.

They'd been such a happy mess. Two broken people, trying to face the world together and be whole.

She didn't want to think they'd been a mistake. After all, they had Junie. Their daughter clearly was the best thing to come out of their marriage. Kylie could overlook the betrayal and heartache for the sake of Junie.

"Kylie." Parker said it gently, almost a question.

"I'm good, just tired of being sick. And don't say it, I know I should have listened to you."

"You are stubborn," Parker said.

Parker swooped Junie up off the bed and gave her bear hugs, and then she sat down in the chair next to the bed, still holding Kylie's daughter. "We're going to keep this girl busy, while you stay busy getting well."

Kylie nodded, fighting tears. When had she last been away from her daughter? Once, maybe, while she and Mark were still married. They'd gone to an award show together. Her best friend in Nashville had let Junie spend the night.

"Don't worry, we will be here to visit. We'll probably go home as soon as the surgery is over and you're in recovery. You won't feel up to visitors."

"I will," Kylie argued.

Parker shook her head, laughing just a little. "No, I promise you won't. But Mark is staying…" She let the words trail off.

"He doesn't have to," Kylie said. "After all, I won't feel like having visitors."

"He doesn't want you to be alone," Matthew said. "For that matter, neither do we. We'll all rest easier, knowing someone is here with you."

"Even if that someone is me?" Mark said as he entered the room, his cowboy hat in his hands, his smile clearly not meant for humor. He looked hurt.

She didn't want to care about his feelings.

"I'm glad you're staying," she assured him out of habit. Just habit, she told herself. She would have been just fine without him at her side.

He gave her a searching look. "Good, because I'm not going anywhere."

"Okay, we're going to say our goodbyes and go back to the waiting room." Parker stood, still holding Junie.

"Okay." Kylie held her arms out for one last hug from her daughter. "I'm going to be just fine."

Junie leaned in to hug her. "I know you are, Mommy. Mark will take care of you."

"Mark." Kylie glanced his way, and he grinned.

"We love you, and we're praying." Parker kissed her cheek, and then she was gone, leaving Matthew and

Mark. The Rivers brothers looked uncomfortable with each other and the situation.

When had they last been in a room together?

"I'm going to pray," Matthew told her as he took her hand. Mark moved to her side and bowed his head, but his hand rested on hers.

The prayer was short but meaningful, bringing tears to her eyes. She'd needed those comforting words. She realized she needed the big brother hug that Matthew gave her before he exited the room, leaving her alone with her ex-husband.

"You really don't have to stay," she said, even as she realized she didn't mean it. As much as she didn't want to admit it, she needed for him to stay.

He'd hurt her, but before that, he'd always been her person.

Mark stayed. No way could he walk away and leave her alone in the hospital. He'd left her on her own one too many times, and this time, he could make the right decision. The decision to be there for her.

As they took her from the room to prepare her for surgery, he clasped her hand and leaned in to place a kiss on her cheek. She closed her eyes, her breath soft as she exhaled.

"I'll be here when you wake up," he promised.

She nodded and a tear squeezed free from beneath closed eyes. He caught it with a brush of his finger across soft skin.

"I'm afraid." Her voice trembled as she made the admission.

Her eyes, dark and shimmering with fear and pain, caught him in a devastating way, almost making him lose his grip on the courage that she needed from him.

"You're going to be fine," he promised. "I'm here, and I'm praying, and you're going to be better in no time."

"It's just a silly appendix," she said with a soft sound of mirth.

"We have to go," the orderly informed them.

"Junie," she rushed their daughter's name as they pushed her away from him.

"She's going to be fine. She's with Matthew and Parker."

"She's six, and she always tries too hard to be strong."

"Like her mother," he said with a wink. "You're going to be okay."

"I know."

And then the orderly pushed the bed through double doors with a sign that prohibited entrance by anyone other than medical personnel.

Mark stood in the hall, unable to walk away, still picturing Kylie's face, pale and exhausted, in pain. He leaned against the wall and waited for the strength to leave, to go find a place to sit and wait. A nurse walked past.

"Will they let me know how she's doing?" he asked.

"And you are?"

"Her husband," he said out of habit. And then he groaned because he wasn't her husband, not anymore, and he had no rights. "Ex-husband. But..."

"Sorry, we can only update if she gave permission."

"I understand, but I'm the only one. Can you find out if she gave permission? Someone has to be here for her." He jerked off his hat and brushed his hand through his tangled curls, wishing that he'd taken time for a haircut. Not that the style of his hair had any importance at the moment.

"You can have a seat in the waiting room," the nurse offered. "And I can check."

He nodded and scooted past her to the small room she indicated. Another waiting room with straight-back, vinyl-covered chairs, a television on low volume and dark windows looking out at a darkened city that he didn't care to see. He wished he'd asked Matthew to stay with him. They hadn't been close in years, but they were still brothers.

Years ago, the four Rivers brothers had been thick as thieves. They'd gone through everything together, and they'd done everything together. Mostly. Matthew, as he'd gotten older, took on the role of keeping them all out of trouble. They hadn't thanked him for that, even though it had been necessary. Someone in the Rivers family had needed to be responsible, and it sure hadn't been their dad, Buck Rivers.

Footsteps in the hall caught his attention. Boots, not the soft-soled shoes of the nurse. He moved away from the window to the coffee pot. As he poured a cup, the newcomer entered.

Not a newcomer. Matthew.

An unexpected feeling of relief swamped him, bringing the burn of unwanted tears. He focused on adding sugar to the hours-old coffee and then creamer that barely made a dint in the dark brew.

A hand touched his shoulder.

"I didn't expect you all to stay," Mark said, his voice catching.

"I sent Parker and Junie on home. They were both worn slick. I couldn't let you do this alone. Plus, I'm the hospital chaplain."

"So you're just here out of a sense of duty?" Mark

picked up his coffee, and then he remembered his manners. "Want a cup?"

"No, thanks. That smells as if it's been here all day. Let me get us a fresh cup. I'll pour that out for you."

"I don't really want coffee," Mark admitted. "I just needed to do something to take my mind off worrying about Kylie."

He left the cup on the table and joined his brother, taking one of the orange vinyl seats that didn't encourage sitting for long.

"I'm here because you're my brother and Kylie is the mother of my niece." Matthew stretched his long legs, crossing them at the ankles. He didn't act at all put off by the furniture.

Mark could admit that he might have been taking his worry out on the chairs. He needed something to focus on, something other than Kylie being sick.

"Thank you," Mark said to his brother, "for being there." He closed his eyes and said another *thank you*, this time to God, for giving him a brother who had a large quantity of forgiveness to pass out to troubled souls.

"No need to thank me."

"I'm sorry," Mark said. "That's why I came home."

"Here to make amends?"

Mark nodded and scrubbed a hand down his face. "Yeah. I guess you probably didn't question why I'd dropped off the face of the earth after last year."

"You did make our wedding memorable." Matthew said it with a chuckle, his dry humor still intact. "And Luke told us where he'd taken you. I waited, hoping you'd call."

"I had to deal with some stuff first. That look on

Junie's face…" He felt another embarrassing sting of tears.

"Yeah, I know." Matthew put a brotherly arm around him and gave him a hard squeeze, then let him go. "We all survived, and it gave us something to talk about."

"I'm guessing it gave the entire town of Sunset Ridge something to talk about." He groaned. "I sang Garth Brooks for you."

"Something like that. Mostly you announced that you didn't mean to ruin our black-tie affair. It didn't sound much like singing."

"That wasn't my best moment, was it? I don't know how to make it up to the two of you, to Junie and to Kylie."

"Mark, we forgive you."

He nodded, stunned, fighting tears and wishing he could be half the man his brother had turned out to be.

"Thank you," he said after getting hold of himself.

"How long are you here for?"

"I guess longer than I'd planned. I can't leave until I know Kylie is okay. She'll need help. I'll be here until arrangements can be made."

"Arrangements?" Matthew asked, his eyes narrowing.

"She'll need help with her shop, with Junie, all the stuff she won't be able to do after surgery."

"Oh, so you're going to hire someone?" The big-brother disapproval came through loud and clear.

"I doubt she'll want my help," he defended.

"You sure of that?"

"Positive. She only took my help tonight because I happened to be there." Mark stood, needing to move away from Matthew and from whatever lecture might be coming. "I need that coffee now."

"Let's go to my office. I can make a fresh pot, and we can talk."

"I don't think I want to talk. I need to find out how she's doing."

"Okay, we'll find out."

"I'm not her next of kin."

Matthew moved him toward the door. "We'll find out how she's doing."

They walked down the hall in the direction of the nurses' station. The nurse saw them coming. She looked up from her computer, smiling at Matthew, frowning at Mark. "I checked the paperwork."

"Is there a way we could find out how much longer?" Matthew asked. "I understand HIPAA. Unfortunately, her only next of kin is a six-year-old child."

"Let me see what I can do," the nurse said as she pushed back from her desk.

"We'll be in my office."

Matthew led Mark down the quiet halls of the hospital. The lights were dim; the rooms were dark. Everything was hushed and somber. He unlocked a door and flipped on the lights. The room they entered had "Parker" touches. The soft, earthy throw rug, the oak desk with the office chair that looked comfortable but antique and two chairs for visitors that looked welcoming in shades of autumn red.

"This is better than the waiting room," Mark acknowledged as he took a seat and watched his brother start the coffee. "*Thank you* is starting to sound repetitive, but it's all I've got."

"You're welcome." Matthew gave him a steady look. "We're brothers. Thick and thin, we're here for each other."

"I know." Mark accepted the cup of coffee, not bothering to add sugar or cream. "I'd forgotten for a bit, but I'm coming back to myself."

"How are you doing?" Matthew asked as he took a seat behind the desk.

"Right now?" Mark sipped the coffee as he searched for the right response. "Right now, I'm holding on by a thread because this day has kind of shaken me. I'm good, though. I'm one year sober, and statistically, if we're looking at statistics, that's important."

"What's the plan for future you?" Matthew asked with a grin.

"Present me. I live in the present. Present me is a one-day-at-a-time person. I don't live in the past, or I try not to. I'm living my present life in hopes that future me is still sober. I'm going to focus on being a better version of myself, a better dad, a better ex-husband."

"Is that what you want?" Matthew asked, delving a little too deeply into things Mark preferred to not deal with.

"Yeah, that's what I want." It was what he trusted himself to do.

The last thing he wanted was to hurt Kylie again. He didn't want to hurt his daughter, either. But the kind of pain and humiliation he put Kylie through, that was something he couldn't do a second time.

He wouldn't. The only way he could guarantee he wouldn't hurt her was to stay out of her life.

A knock on the door interrupted the conversation.

"Come in," Matthew offered.

The nurse stepped into the room. "She's out of surgery. The doctor is coming down to update you. She appointed you as a contact person, but also gave permission for you to make decisions if she is unable to."

The nurse left, and a few minutes later, the doctor

found them. He gave Mark a tired smile as he stood in the doorway to address them.

"She's okay?" Mark stood, ready to go to her.

"She will be." Dr. Janson sighed. "She's fortunate that you brought her in tonight, or it could have been worse. We're looking at a pretty bad infection from the bacteria of the ruptured appendix. She's a sick young woman with a long road ahead of her. I'm hoping we can have her home by midweek, but it'll depend on how she responds to the antibiotics."

"Can I see her?"

"Soon," Dr. Janson answered.

The doctor left. Mark sat back down, feeling frazzled, useless and now exhausted.

"It's okay to feel overwhelmed. We all get that way sometimes."

"I know," Mark responded. He felt more than overwhelmed. He felt wound tight on the inside. The old Mark would have been searching for a drink. New Mark focused on taking a few steady breaths, and he said a prayer for peace.

"What are you going to do?" Matthew asked. The question meant something.

Mark closed his eyes, thinking of all his plans. He'd come here with every intention of leaving in just a matter of days. It was Thursday. He wanted to be back in Nashville by Sunday.

"What is that verse in Isaiah? 'My thoughts are not your thoughts, neither are your ways my ways, saith the Lord.'" Mark found himself laughing a little at the irony of his plans being interrupted.

Matthew also chuckled. "Isaiah 55:8. Verse 9 is also recommended. 'For as the heavens are higher than the earth, so are my ways higher than your ways, and my thoughts than your thoughts.'"

"Nice," Mark said. "Thanks for the reminder."

"God's word, not mine," Matthew reminded. "Plans change, Mark. Sometimes the plan and our path change at the same time."

"I'm not sure if she'll want me to stay," he admitted. "She has a lot of good reasons for not wanting me in her life."

"I know that Junie wants you here. She was worried you'd leave and not tell her goodbye."

Mark closed his eyes for a moment, just long enough to regroup.

"When you go home, tell her I'm not going anywhere yet."

"I'll let her know. And you should go check on Kylie."

"Thanks for the talk."

"That's what big brothers are for, to give unsolicited advice."

Mark hugged his brother, and then he left to go find Kylie. His plans had changed, but that didn't mean this new plan didn't have merit. Kylie needed him. He needed to be a better version of himself. For her. For Junie. For his future.

Chapter Three

Mark left the hospital in the middle of the night. Kylie had insisted he should go get some sleep so she could sleep and so he'd be able to check on Junie. He drove her car back to Sunset Ridge and parked it in front of her shop, then he climbed into his old truck that smelled of age, motor oil and the farm, and he drove to the Rocking R. He realized one thing on the drive to the ranch: the truck didn't have much of a heater.

The old farmhouse he'd grown up in lay in silence. Not one light had been left on. Of course, Buck hadn't been expecting company.

Frozen, he searched the front porch, knowing Buck always kept a key hidden. He overturned planters, moved rugs and looked under the cushions of the patio furniture that looked newer than anything Buck had ever had on that old front porch.

No key. Since when did Buck lock doors and not leave a spare key? He stood on the porch, trying to think of another hiding spot. The porch light came on, and the door opened. Buck stepped out, wearing flannel pajamas and pointing a shotgun.

Mark raised his hands and stepped back. "Hey, whoa, hold on, Buck, it's me, Mark."

Buck lowered the weapon and stepped a little closer, peering at his son as if he'd just spotted a cockroach in the kitchen. "What are you doing out here making all that ruckus? Some people are trying to sleep."

"I was looking for a key. I needed a place to sleep."

"Get in here." Buck waved the gun in the direction of the front door.

"Do you think you could put that shotgun down?"

"It ain't loaded."

"Then what good is it doing you?"

"Scared you, didn't it?"

"Yeah," Mark admitted. "It scared me. Mind if I go to sleep?"

"I guess I don't mind. You could at least say hello and tell me why you're here bothering me."

"I didn't plan on bothering you. I had to take Kylie to the hospital tonight. I'll be sticking around until I know she's okay."

"What's the matter with her?"

"Appendix." Mark scrubbed a hand across his face. "Could we talk in the morning?"

Buck pursed his lips. "Well, that's a shame. She's a good gal. I guess you can tell me more tomorrow morning."

"Yes, we can talk tomorrow." He was exhausted, and the conversation was buzzing around in his head. "I'm tired."

"I'm sure you are. Well, you know where your room is."

"Thanks, Buck."

"Yep, you're welcome." Buck headed down the hall,

tall and stooped but healthier than he'd been in years. Sobriety did that for a person.

Mark didn't bother turning on lights. He knew his way to the room he'd slept in as a kid. He kicked off his boots and climbed into the bed, the lumps and bumps of the mattress familiar and strangely comforting. He pulled the quilt that smelled of time and dust up to his chin and went to sleep.

Hours later, or maybe ten minutes, he woke up to sunshine streaming through the room and foul breath heating his face. He pushed at the interloper, and the dog gave a soft woof. "Go away, you mutt."

The dog jumped off the bed and padded across the room to the open door. He woofed again, as if commanding Mark to get out of bed.

"I'll get up when I feel like getting up," he growled at the gray-and-white Australian shepherd. "Where'd you come from anyway?"

The dog sat down and gave him a wise look. He didn't like the look, not this early in the morning. A man didn't want to feel as if he'd been outsmarted by a canine.

The smell of chocolate and something baked came drifting through the open door. The dog didn't hold much sway over Mark, but his empty stomach did. The growling and rumbling pushed him from the bed, still in the clothes he'd been wearing for two days. He guessed he probably stunk as much as the cattle dog. He'd best take care of that before he headed down to breakfast.

A quick shower and change of clothes and he was ready to greet the day. He found the dog waiting in the hallway.

"Let's go." Mark gave a soft whistle, and the dog followed him down the stairs. The aroma of chocolate grew stronger.

He walked through the house to the kitchen. Buck's kitchen, always a surprise. The chef's kitchen with the fancy cabinets and granite countertops had been installed almost thirty years ago, something Buck had done to try and keep his city-bred, country-club loving wife. Mark didn't call her Mom any more than he called Buck, Dad. But Buck had definitely earned the title of Father more than Isabel Rivers had earned the right to be called Mother.

At least Izzy had done right by the youngest Rivers child, Jael. The only girl had been born after Izzy left Buck. And Luke Rivers. The third of the four boys had sold out and moved to Tulsa to live with their mother. He'd waited until the rest of them had fled the state, but he'd gone to her, and now he helped run her family business.

Traitor.

The same traitor that had hauled Mark to rehab. For that, he'd be eternally grateful, even if he never found a way to get along with his little brother.

Sitting at the counter, perched on a barstool that seemed particularly large for a small child, sat his daughter. Junie was stirring something in a bowl she could barely see over the top of. She had a dab of chocolate on her face, and a grin split her dimpled cheeks in a merry way. She was the stuff that country songs about babies and puppies were made of.

"Hey, June Bug, I didn't expect to see you here." He started to give her a hug, but then wondered if she would even want one from him. "Mind if I give you a hug?"

Her eyes narrowed, and she made a face. "I like hugs."

He hugged her.

"What are you making?"

"Grandpa Buck is making chocolate chocolate-chip pancakes. They're my favorite. I get to stir."

"And eat chocolate while stirring?" he asked. She nodded.

"Coffee?" Buck asked.

"Sure thing." He rounded the counter and found a coffee cup already next to the coffeemaker. "Thanks. I didn't mean to sleep this late."

"It's just eight in the morning. You didn't sleep long at all." Buck wiped his hands on a towel and reached for the bowl that Junie had been stirring. "Let's see what we can do. We already have chocolate-chip muffins ready. They're on the cooling rack."

"Did you turn into a chef?" Mark asked as he grabbed a muffin so filled with chocolate chips he could barely see the cake. This explained the chocolate on his daughter's face.

"I had to do something to keep myself busy. I recommend baking—it's soothing."

Soothing? He couldn't remember ever hearing his dad use that word before. Not once. Ever.

Buck had never been a soother, more of a "pull yourself up by the bootstraps, shake it off and don't cry" kind of man. Being sober and having grandchildren had changed him.

Not in a bad way.

The muffins were mighty tasty.

Pancake batter sizzled on the griddle. "Why don't you grab the can of whipped topping out of the fridge," Buck ordered while focusing on cooking.

"Can do."

Junie cleared her throat and both Mark and Buck gave her a quick look. "What's up, June Bug?" Mark asked.

"I'd like to see my mom," she replied in a matter-of-fact voice that only hinted at tears.

"We'll finish our breakfast, take care of any chores your grandpa has for us and then we'll go see her."

"Is she going to be okay?" Junie asked, her voice holding a little more of a quiver.

"She's going to be just fine," he assured her. "She's going to take some time to recover, which means not working, but she'll get strong and soon be right back to making you do your schoolwork."

Her little nose wrinkled. "I like school."

"I'm glad you do."

"You'll have to help me until she gets better." Junie said it with a doubtful expression.

"I, uh…" Now what did he say to that?

"You're not staying, are you?" She sniffled, but put on a brave face, a face that should have made her grandpa happy and not had him glaring at Mark. "It's okay. I can manage."

"You don't have to manage on your own," he assured her. He was really out of practice at this parenting thing. He'd visited in the years since Kylie left him, took their daughter and hightailed it back home. He hadn't parented.

He hadn't drawn the connections before, but he guessed that made him a lot like Izzy. His mother had become a visitor in their lives, not a parent. She hadn't been able to manage four wild Rivers boys and their father.

Izzy liked to manage. He guessed they differed there. He liked to avoid trouble and sometimes he avoided responsibility. Those were two things he planned on getting better at.

"Pancakes are ready," Buck said in a stilted tone that

clearly conveyed his disapproval of his son. He put a plate in front of Junie, glared at Mark and went back to the griddle to pour more batter on the nonstick surface.

Step up and be the dad, his conscience told him. What if he couldn't? What if he failed and let her down?

But wouldn't he be failing her if he left and didn't help?

"Junie, I'll be here to help you with your homework. Until your mom is on her feet and able to take care of things, I'll be here."

"Hmmph," from Buck.

Mark brushed a hand through his still tangled curls and tried to gather his thoughts and skills as a parent.

"We're going to be fine. Your mom is going to be fine."

"Am I staying with you?" Junie asked. "Or Aunt Parker? She dropped me off because she had to work and so does Uncle Matthew. They have Faith. You're her uncle, but you haven't met her."

The baby girl, Faith. No, Mark hadn't met her, but he knew the story. About eighteen months earlier, the little girl had been abandoned in the back of Matthew's truck. Newborn, fighting for her life, and her mom, fighting her own poor odds, had left her to be found by someone who would care for her.

His thoughts had meandered like a kid on a country road. He realized that both Buck and Junie were staring at him, waiting for some kind of response.

"Oh, yes, of course you can stay with me." His heart gave a hard thump at the thought. There were so many ways he could mess this up, and she was the one reason to not mess up.

"Okay, that's settled," she said with a tilt of her chin.

"Now we need to figure out the coffee shop. Someone is going to have to open that place up."

"I'm sure it'll be fine until your mom is up and around."

She gave him a hard stare and then proceeded to tell him why it wouldn't be okay for the coffee shop to remain closed. He listened, heartsick at the explanation about her grandma Mindy and the help she needed to be well. Of course Kylie provided the money and the help. Of course she needed the coffee shop up and running.

For years, Kylie had been his best friend. He'd promised to make her life better, to protect her, to cherish her. He'd let her down in so many ways.

Kylie blinked a few times and then opened her eyes to see a little face peering into hers. She smiled and reached to touch her daughter's precious face.

"Mommy," Junie whispered, and then she cried.

"Oh, honey, I'm here and I'm okay. I promise you I'm going to be just fine."

Junie climbed into the bed with her, and Kylie didn't object, even though it hurt like fire to have her daughter curled against her side. She leaned in, pressing her lips to Junie's curly, dark hair. She glanced at the man who stood awkwardly near the window, not really a part of their lives and yet, somehow, a part of their current situation.

She was torn. She wanted him here because he'd always been with her in the hard times. She wanted him gone because she didn't want to start relying on him, only to have him walk away. Or worse.

"How are you doing?" he asked. "Are you in pain? Do you need anything?"

He was unsure, she realized. His confidence had

taken a beating. It showed in his eyes, in the way he shifted and fidgeted. Once upon a time, she would have found his uncertainty cute. She could no longer care for him. She just couldn't allow herself to feel. Not for him.

"I'm doing okay," she assured him. "I have to get up and walk."

"Why?"

"They want me to keep moving." She didn't want to move. She wanted to stay still. Now she wanted to cuddle with Junie and pretend everything was okay. She wasn't okay. She was very sick. Weak and shaky with a fever that came and went.

"Let me help," he offered.

"Help me walk?"

"Of course." He smiled down at Junie. "Keep the bed warm?"

Junie nodded and curled up on her side, reaching for the remote. "I'll watch television."

Kylie didn't want his help. She didn't want to hold his hand and lean on him. How could she say no? He was there, at her side, holding her as she slid out of the bed, pushed her feet into the hospital slippers and pulled closed the robe that Parker had brought in a bag that morning. Parker always thought about the little things. A soft nightgown, a robe, sweatpants and T-shirts, toiletries. And chocolate.

There were roses, too. Those had been sent by Mark. The over-the-top bouquet had arrived just before he'd shown up with Junie. Roses, baby's breath and daisies. She understood the combination. He'd always said she was his classy country girl—daisies and roses, diamonds and turquoise.

"Take my arm," he told her as they walked. "Why the walking?"

"To make sure I stay moving. I don't need blood clots on top of this infection."

"Gotcha," he said.

They walked. She leaned against him, thankful that he was strong when she felt weak. He smelled good, too. A mixture of the outdoors, expensive cologne and minty toothpaste. She pushed away the memories of the two of them, how they'd made each other better, stronger. That had been a long time ago. They hadn't been together for several years, and it had been even longer since they'd been good together.

"I know," he said after they'd made one trip down the corridor. "I know."

What did he know?

"I'm sorry, what?"

"Junie is worried about the coffee shop being closed," he told her, his voice hesitant.

"The coffee shop will be fine," she assured him.

"The money you get for child support and alimony. She said it goes into an account for her, a trust. And it goes to a home for her grandmother, Mindy."

This wasn't the conversation she wanted to have, not today. Maybe not ever. It had stopped being his business. Except now, Junie had made it his business.

"Mark, she's my mother." Not that she owed him explanations. "Junie doesn't go without. I don't take from what you send for her."

"I know that." He sighed, the sound filled with frustration. "I know she's your mom, and I know you wouldn't take from Junie. It's just that I think of how she treated you and the danger she put you in."

"I can't punish her for being an addict."

They both faltered as they walked the hall. She felt his footsteps hesitate. Hers also slowed. They clung to one another, and she didn't want to cling. She couldn't undo their past, either, pretending it had never happened. Junie lived as proof of the love they'd shared. Junie was the reason Kylie needed real boundaries between herself and this man—because he'd devastated them once, and he could so easily do it again.

She wouldn't allow Junie to live the life she'd lived with her own mother. Speaking of Mindy brought it all back, reminding her of the reasons she'd left him.

"I'm sorry," he said. "I would have given you more had I known you were paying for her home. I'll take care of it from this point on."

"It's my responsibility," she argued.

"I know that I can't be the husband you deserve, but I can at least be a friend. Let me be that for you and let me take care of the cost of the home. Is it an apartment?"

She shook her head, again, near tears. Her legs were weak, and her body ached. She made the slow turn back to her room, trying to order her thoughts, to think about how it would work out if he were her friend.

She knew they couldn't go back, but going forward, perhaps they could build a relationship that benefited their daughter and made it easier for them to communicate.

"It's an apartment in an assisted living facility for people who can live on their own but with daily help," she explained. "It's important that she is cared for. She is damaged, Mark. She's always been damaged. I don't know how I survived her, but she didn't survive her parents. It's a cycle that I don't want to repeat."

"I know." He kept a strong arm around her, supporting her. She relaxed, allowing herself to feel comforted by his nearness. "We will figure this out, Kylie.

I'll make sure everything is paid for. I don't want you to worry. I just want you to take time to get healthy."

"I don't want you to feel as if you're responsible for this. I have the coffee shop, and I can afford to care for my mother."

"Stop being stubborn," he told her with that charming grin of his. "I want to help you. I owe you so much."

She took that back, the charming part. The grin, the expression, had changed. He wasn't carefree, charming the world with his music and his smiles. His eyes wore the tired expression of someone who had fallen hard. He also cared. No matter what had happened between them, he cared about her, about his daughter. He just hadn't been good at showing them that side of himself.

Maybe someday they'd be friends again. She might like it if that happened. He'd been a good friend.

"I'm going to hire someone to help at the coffee shop," he told her. All of her warm fuzzy feelings evaporated. "I stopped by and put up a sign."

"You can't do that. It's my coffee shop."

"And you want to keep it going. You're not going to be able to open, and you told me the town is planning a special Valentine's Day celebration."

"They are, we are. I can still do this."

"In a month, or however long it is until this festival, you think you can be healthy and able to do this on your own?"

She pulled free from his arms and nearly collapsed in the chair near the window. Her body trembled from the exertion of the short walk down the hall. Mark grabbed the extra blanket, folded at the bottom of the bed, and shook it loose to drape over her.

"Valentine's Day in Sunset Ridge," she explained. "It's another project to bring people to town. A tent on the square with lights and live music. A special dinner at Chuck's, also at my place. There will be vendors with different treats and crafts."

"I'll do what I can to help," he assured her.

"Thank you," she said.

"That wasn't so hard, now was it?" Junie said it from her place on the bed, a giggle punctuating the statement. She remained glued to the television, but she'd obviously been listening.

"Now where did you learn that?" Mark asked his daughter as he picked her up, tickling her until she belly laughed.

"From my grandpa Buck. He says it every time I do a chore for him."

"Grandpa Buck, huh?" Mark looked surprised, and for a moment, something like anger flashed in his eyes. "I'm glad he's teaching you to do some chores."

"Did he teach you chores?" Junie asked, all six-year-old innocence and trust.

"In a way," Mark answered. Buck hadn't really taught his boys; he'd just expected them to do what needed to be done. Junie didn't need those stories.

"Did he make you chocolate-chip pancakes?" Junie continued, unaware.

"He didn't. He made other things, though,"

"Like what?" Junie remained in his arms, her arms around his neck, her head back to watch as he replied.

"Hmmm, let me think." Mark paused for a moment, and then he grinned. "He made a pretty decent fried bologna sandwich. Matthew made the pancakes."

"Did you cook?" Junie quizzed, unwilling to let go of her father and the stories of his childhood.

"I did," Mark said with a grin and a wink. "Grilled peanut butter and jelly."

"What is that?"

"I'll make you one. Maybe if we can't find help for the coffee shop, we'll just open up and make grilled PB and J with coffee."

Junie laughed at that. "Daddy, you're silly. I'm glad you came home."

"Me, too."

Kylie watched the two of them, father and daughter, so very much alike. Their conversation, carefree and sweet for Junie, brought complications for Mark and Kylie. She realized the implication of what her daughter had said. At six, she didn't see the heartache coming. When Mark left, there would be a hole. Their daughter would have to miss him all over again.

She should say something to prepare Junie for the day he would leave, but the words stuck in a throat tight with emotion. Mark gave her a quick look; perhaps she'd made a noise of protest. She managed to compose herself, and she kept her misgivings to herself. Mark was Junie's father. No matter what had happened in their marriage, Junie deserved a daddy who would be there for her, making her laugh and keeping her safe.

Kylie wished she could believe in his ability to be that person. Their marriage might be over, but she wanted him to be the father Junie needed.

Chapter Four

The sun was a red glow on the eastern horizon when Mark parked in front of Kylie's Coffee Shop and Bakery the Tuesday following Kylie's surgery. In the seat next to him, Junie roused, her eyes still sleepy and her hair tangled. She yawned big.

Man, he loved his daughter. It had taken six years, a broken marriage and a lot of therapy for him to grasp just what his little girl meant to him. No man should have to go that path to realize what mattered most.

Some people, he guessed, did have to go through the wilderness in order to find their promised land. If only he'd realized everything he really wanted had been right there in front of him and he just hadn't recognized it.

Too late, he told himself. He'd realized too late. Now, he knew he couldn't go back. He couldn't claim them as his, because the uncertainties of life frightened him too much. What if he failed them again? The thought made him want to run for the hills.

He'd accepted that they were better off without him. If he kept reminding himself of that, maybe leaving wouldn't hurt so much.

"I don't think you can do this on your own," Junie

told him, with all of the wisdom of a six-year-old. She had sleepy eyes and a blanket for comfort, but a dimpled grin that wouldn't allow him to remain in the dumps.

"I'm willing to try," he assured her. He had to try. Kylie had made it pretty obvious she wouldn't take more money, so the only other option was to make sure she didn't lose income while she recuperated.

He would hire someone as soon as possible, but until then, he was the hired hand.

They entered the building, and he immediately kicked up the heat. Junie hunkered down in her coat and pulled a portable heater out from under the counter.

"You can plug this in until it gets warmer. I always sit by this and wait."

"Okay, let's get you warm and then I'll figure things out from here." Mark plugged in the heater and turned it on high. Junie pulled a stool back a safe distance and sat down.

"You have to start the coffeemaker."

"Of course, coffeemaker. I can make coffee."

"It isn't just making coffee," Junie said with a knowing tilt to her chin. "It's fresh roasted from a place in Tulsa. And Mommy knows all kind of tricks with syrups and frothy milk and sometimes cocoa sprinkled on top."

"It does sound fancy," Mark admitted. He was used to coffee from a can that he scooped into the coffeemaker he and Kylie had purchased soon after he got his first real paycheck in the music business.

"Sometimes Mommy makes Cuban coffee. I sip it from little cups she bought online." Junie reached under the counter and pulled out the dainty little cups. "Oh, my schoolwork is in there. Should I get that out, too?"

Coffee, schoolwork, all the little day-to-day things that he'd missed out on. The things he had no clue about.

All of the things Kylie had been handling on her own. Guilt tasted bitter in his mouth, but he didn't have time to dwell on it, not with Junie staring up at him, waiting for answers.

"Schoolwork is a good idea." He was studying the coffeemaker, but he caught the look his daughter gave him. She knew he didn't know a thing about parenting, or about coffee. The machine in front of him seemed a lot more complicated than the discount-brand one he'd kept all these years, even though it was starting to clog up and make monster-under-the-bed kind of noises. "About this coffeemaker…"

Junie giggled as she watched him study the gadgets and buttons. "It's complicated."

"It's very complicated. I'm not sure if I can even pronounce the brand." He searched the small kitchen area and found bins of coffee, filters, cabinets of syrups and a cooler filled with all types of creamers.

His daughter moved a little closer to his side. "I'm not allowed to work it because it has very hot water, but I've watched Mommy. You push that button. And see, it makes espresso." She pointed to a button. "It also makes regular brewed coffee."

He saw the switch for that.

"Mommy also makes pour-over coffee and cold brew."

"I might have to stick to espresso and regular brewed coffee for now. I'm not a skilled barista."

The door dinged, and their first customer walked in, a lady in a straight skirt and no-frills blouse with sleek, dark hair. "Is the coffee ready? Where's Kylie?"

"She's sick," Junie offered. "Hi, Mrs. Potter. We're just getting ready to make coffee. This is my daddy."

"Why, it certainly is. Mr. Rivers, it's good to have you in Sunset Ridge."

"Thank you, but hold the applause because I'm not sure how this coffee will work out for us."

"Do you have any of Kylie's quiche? I like the crust-less."

Mark turned to Junie because, for now, she was running this show. She winked and hopped down off the stool. "I got this, Mark."

"Mark?" he called out to her.

"Dad," she called back.

She returned a moment later with a box; his tiny girl with her dark curls in a tight ponytail, compliments of Aunt Parker, had everything under control. "The quiche are in here. You have to put them in the microwave, and they don't cook for very long because they're eggs and eggs are sensitive."

"Sensitive," he repeated. He should have asked Kylie for a list of things to do here. But asking for a list would have meant telling her that he planned on trying to open for her.

"You can't cook them very long, or they get gross," Junie explained.

"Do you know how long?"

The coffeemaker had stopped, and he poured a cup for the customer. She gave it a serious look, sniffed and shrugged.

"If the quiche is a problem, I can make do with a muffin."

So could he, but he didn't have a clue about muffins.

"I think we can figure out the quiche."

He gave his daughter a questioning look, and she just shrugged and dug a quiche out of the box. She wore gloves that were too large.

"Any hints?" he whispered.

"I'm six," Junie told him in an exaggerated whisper. "I can't even ride my bike without training wheels."

The customer giggled.

"Okay, I've got this," he said with more confidence than he felt. "Do we have other food in the freezer?"

"A few things. Mommy usually bakes over the week-end."

She hopped down from the stool and hurried to the back, where the coolers and freezer were located. Mark peeked in at the quiche and waited for the microwave to stop.

When he'd been in rehab, they'd encouraged him to try something new. They'd suggested college classes or a hobby, something to refocus his energies, something other than just the obvious return to his career. They wanted him to challenge himself and also find ways to deal with stress. He'd never been a peaceful person. He'd always been high energy, chasing dreams and running from his past.

By "try something new," he doubted the therapists had meant for him to take on a coffee shop and bakery.

The smell of the overly sensitive eggs filled the air. It wasn't a pleasant aroma, and if he had to guess, he'd cooked the eggs too long. He glanced at the customer, and the look on her face wavered somewhere between sympathy and disgust.

"I think I'll have to pass on the quiche this morning. But the coffee is decent. How much do I owe you?"

"That one is on me," Mark told her. "Come back again, and I promise I'll have this figured out."

Now he knew, two minutes was too long for a frozen crustless quiche. The only way to work this out was to try another and heat it in short spurts of time. He could do this. After all, it was just a quiche.

Junie returned. "There are six muffins and five scones. That won't last long. We have to find someone who can bake."

And then her little face dimpled, and her gray eyes lit with mischief.

"What?" Did he really want to know?

"We could make muffins!" she informed him with a frightening level of excitement.

"I don't know," he told her, aware of a flash of disappointment overshadowing her excitement. Baking definitely didn't top the list of hobbies he thought he'd like to try. Although his dad had said it was soothing. Whatever that meant.

The look on Junie's face, equal parts hopeful and disappointed, that look might encourage a guy to put on an apron and try his hand at baking.

The front door opened, and a group of ladies entered. They zeroed in on him with bright expressions.

"Mr. Rivers," the leader started, "I'm Marla Goode, and these two lovely ladies are my friends, Lena Pratt and Pearl Fedders. We are members of the Community Betterment and Growth Committee. If it's easier, you can refer to us as the committee." She gave him a quick smile and hurried on as if she feared he might interrupt or kick them out. "Kylie is a member of our group, as are several other local business owners. As longtime residents, we are working to preserve our small town."

"I see." He didn't, but he could guess that the introduction would end in some type of sales pitch. "I'm sure you know that Kylie is recovering."

"We are aware," said Mrs. Goode. "As soon as she is home, we will have a meal train ready to provide food. But until she's better, we were hoping you could help us with our February Sweethearts in Sunset. Isn't that catchy? We will have special meals at our eating establishments, a venue with twinkly lights, music and dancing, also craft vendors and a flower truck."

"Sounds to me like it's all planned. If you need a donation, I'll gladly help."

"It's planned, but we still have much to accomplish in the next month." This came from the taller lady in the business suit, Pearl, her short hair cropped and curly. "We need to finalize the menus for each restaurant and assign a committee to arrange the decorating of our dance venue."

"Dance venue?" He couldn't help but be curious.

"The old bank on the corner of the square," Lena Pratt responded. He remembered Lena. She lived in a big old house on the edge of town. As far as he knew, she'd never married, and her money came from a family trust.

"I'm still not sure how I can help," he said.

"We just need someone to help with a few things that had been on Kylie's list." This from Marla Goode.

"I'm afraid I won't be here." He shrugged as he said it. The last thing he wanted was to be on a committee with a bunch of women organizing an event for a town he'd said goodbye to sixteen years ago.

"Kylie will be out of the hospital in a day or two, and by the first of next week, I'll be heading back to Nashville."

As he said the last part, he glanced at Junie and watched as her expression fell. She blinked furiously and swiped away a tear that trickled down her cheek. He'd done it again. He didn't want this to be the relationship he had with his daughter. He didn't want to be like his father, always hurting the people who depended on him.

More than anything, he wanted to be Junie and Kylie's hero. He'd just never been hero material.

The room had grown smaller since she'd been admitted to the hospital five days earlier. Smaller, more confining, the bed more uncomfortable and the food less palatable. Kylie knew she was becoming a difficult patient. She just wanted to go home. She wanted to be with her daughter. She wanted to be in her coffee shop, visiting with her customers and making people happy with her baked goods.

The door opened, and she sat up, hopeful. And then she sighed and hunkered back down, pulling up the recently heated blanket.

"Sorry to disappoint you," Parker said. Parker, the woman who would have been her sister in-law, had Kylie and Mark remained married.

Matthew and Parker Rivers still claimed Kylie and Junie as family. They were her only family, because her mother, Mindy, was less capable now than she'd been twenty years go and the Duncans had never claimed her.

"I'm not disappointed. I'm just tired of being here."

Parker sat at the edge of the bed. "How do you feel?"

"Better today than yesterday. Now, I'm worried about Junie, worried about my business and the Valentine's Day event in town. I have so much to get done, and I can't stand being stuck here."

"All of that can wait," Parker told her in typical matter-of-fact Parker fashion. "And Mark will bring Junie in later. He's doing a good job, Kylie. She's safe, and she's having fun with Mark and Buck."

"Thank you," she whispered, and then she embarrassed herself by crying. The tears trickled at first, but then picked up steam as she tried to explain herself. It was serious ugly crying, but she couldn't stop.

Parker grabbed a tissue out of the box on the table and handed it to her. Fortunately, Parker didn't hug her; that would have taken the crying to another level.

After a few minutes, Kylie pulled herself together.

"I need to go home," Kylie repeated. "I know he can take care of her, but she'll…"

She didn't want to say it. She didn't want to be unfair to Mark or to Junie.

"He won't stay," Parker filled in. "That's why you're worried."

Kylie nodded and dabbed at a few stray tears.

"It isn't as if I want him to stay." She felt she had to explain. "He's been out of our lives, and we're used to the way things are now. I want him in Junie's life. It's important for both of them. I just don't want her life, and her emotions, in turmoil. I want structure. Ugh, I'm a mess. I just need structure."

Because structure had been sadly missing in her own childhood and teen years. She wanted it for herself and her daughter. She wanted to know that their home was a safe space, there would be food on the table, the electric bill would always get paid and there wouldn't be chaos. There wouldn't be emotional rages and intoxicated meltdowns.

"I understand," Parker said. "You're a great mom, Kylie. You're giving Junie what she needs."

"I hope so."

"Have they given you any idea when you can go home?" Parker asked, changing the subject.

"Maybe tomorrow. They're doing more bloodwork. I've been fever free since yesterday, and I've finished the antibiotics."

"That's all good," Parker acknowledged. "The last thing you want is to go home and then have a setback."

The door opened, and the conversation ended. Kylie brushed away any remaining traces of her tears as Junie raced to the bed and climbed in, careful not to bump her. Kylie wrapped her arms around her daughter, needing to hold her just as much as Junie needed to be held. She leaned in, sniffing Junie's dark curls and the familiar scent of their lavender shampoo.

"How did you get here? Did you drive yourself?" Kylie teased.

Junie laughed. "No silly, Daddy brought me. But he told me to come on up. He had to do something."

Kylie pushed aside negative suspicions.

"What have you been doing today? I expected you earlier."

"We were working," Junie explained. "I got my schoolwork caught up. Daddy isn't as bad at homeschooling as he thought he'd be. And we decorated, and I taught him to make coffee, but he…"

"Hey, don't tell all of our secrets," Mark said from the doorway, where he stood with a bouquet of roses.

"Oh, are there secrets?" Kylie asked, laughing as she tickled Junie in an attempt to free the secrets. Or perhaps she needed a distraction because Mark looked so good. He looked like the man she'd married, just older. Older, more mature, more attractive. He still had the too-long dark hair that had a penchant for curls, the laughing gray eyes that sometimes looked more like silver. Worse, he had that grin, the dimpled grin that undid her common sense.

"We burned the quiche and sold all the muffins, but Daddy can't make very good coffee."

"On that, I'm out of here." Parker leaned in to give her a quick hug and included Junie in the embrace.

Kylie watched her friend scurry from the room, and then she allowed herself to make eye contact with Mark. He stood just inside the room with the hospital bouquet in his hands. It was the typical glass bud vase, three yellow roses with baby's breath and a bright pink ribbon tied in a bow. He gave her a shy smile.

The smile took her back to their childhood and the little boy who welcomed her on that scary first day of school at Sunset Ridge Elementary. They'd fled Oklahoma City to escape her mother's abusive boyfriend, and they'd somehow managed to rent a tiny trailer in the local trailer park. Now she knew the money came from Roger Duncan, her father.

When they'd moved in, Kylie had been so happy. It had been safe and one of the nicer places they'd lived in. Her mom had made promises to eight-year-old Kylie, promises of a better life, of getting clean, of having food and clothes like everyone else. It was going to be so much better, Mindy had promised. It hadn't been her first promise, or the first promise broken.

"Aren't the flowers pretty?" Junie asked the question, dragging Kylie back. "They were for a baby, but Daddy asked the lady to take off the big baby balloon."

Mark's eyes crinkled at the corners, and Kylie felt a little lighter. All because Junie couldn't keep a secret.

"They're beautiful." She hugged her daughter close, loving her so much. "You've had a busy morning."

"Uh-oh," he said with a dimpled grin. "Are we in trouble?"

She shook her head. "As long as I still have a business."

"We didn't do too much damage," he assured her as

he set the vase of flowers on the table next to her bed. He needed to stop buying flowers. As if he knew her thoughts, he winked, stopping her objections. "Junie helped me pick these out, and she was a big help at the coffee shop."

"You don't have to do this."

"Kylie, while I'm here, I'm going to help."

A soft knock on the door interrupted the conversation. Kylie called out for the visitor to enter. Dr. Janson entered the room, peering over the top of his black, wire-framed glasses. His smile, kind and reassuring. Fatherly.

"Mrs. Rivers, it's good to see you all here together. I wanted to bring good news before I leave for the day."

Mrs. Rivers. She started to correct him, but chose not to, not with Junie present.

"I like good news." Kylie sat up a little straighter, pushing aside thoughts of being Mrs. Rivers.

"Me, too," Junie chimed in.

Dr. Janson chuckled. "Well, I'm glad you like good news. I also hope you like going home. I'm going to release you today, but only if you have someone to stay with you."

She hesitated, relieved by the news but then worried about the "someone to stay with you" part. Who could she call? She couldn't drag Parker away from work and her family. She could possibly call one of the retired ladies from church. Maybe Lena.

"I'll take care of her," Mark jumped in to offer.

She gave him a quick look, then glanced at their daughter. Junie's face lit up.

"We can take you to Grandpa Buck's house. He's a real good cook. You can sleep upstairs in the spare room with me." Junie appeared ready to rattle on with her plan, but something in Kylie's expression must have stopped her. Whatever else she planned on saying faded away, and she bit down on her bottom lip.

"I'll be fine. And I have Junie."

"I know you'll be fine," Dr. Janson stated, his smile gone. "I have to insist that you can't be on your own for a day or two. I know that Junie is a wonderful nurse, but she's going to need help."

She wanted to go home. Kylie held her daughter close and, over her head, met Mark's steady gaze. He gave a slight nod.

"If we're at Buck's, Parker is close by if we need her." Mark made it seem like the logical choice.

She wasn't so sure, but she didn't have the strength to argue.

"Thank you," Kylie said. "We'll go to Buck's with Mark."

"That's good," Dr. Janson said as he typed something into his phone. "I'm sure they'll take good care of you. Call my office tomorrow and make an appointment because I want to see you at the end of the week. A nurse will be in with your paperwork. I know that you think you're released and you should be able to pack your bag and walk out, but remember, nothing in a hospital moves that quickly. Give them an hour."

An hour. She was going home; she could handle an hour of waiting. No, take that back, she was going with Mark and Junie to Buck's house. It wasn't the end of the world, she told herself. She could handle being with Mark for the next few days.

Chapter Five

The wait for the paperwork seemed to take forever. Kylie knew it was just over an hour, but it felt more like ten. Eventually a nurse brought it and they were able to leave. Kylie found herself in the passenger seat of Mark's truck. Junie sat buckled between them, occasionally looking from one of her parents to the other. Kylie could guess her daughter's thoughts. A combination of hope and worry were darkening her eyes as she studied them. Kylie understood because she'd been a child always hoping, praying, for some stability in her life.

Kylie had given her daughter stability by leaving Mark in Nashville and starting a new life in Sunset Ridge. She sometimes worried what God thought of her because she'd walked out on her marriage, on her vows. She'd had to forgive herself for that, and she knew God wasn't holding it over her head like an angry parent, waiting to punish her for bad behavior. She'd done her best to protect herself and Junie.

She hadn't walked away without trying to help her husband. She'd prayed. She'd tried to reconcile. She'd begged him to get help. She'd already lived that life with her mother. She hadn't wanted to live it with her husband. She hadn't wanted Junie to live that life.

Mark had been in a place too dark to reach. He'd been too caught up in himself and in the bottle.

Yet here they were, together. She gave him a quick look. Heat rushed to her cheeks because he chose the same moment to glance her way. It still tied them together, the chemistry, the knowing each other better than they'd ever known anyone else.

He was better. She could see it in his eyes. For his sake, she hoped he stayed better. For Junie's sake.

"Thank you, for being here. I know this wasn't in your plans."

"It wasn't, but an appendectomy wasn't in yours, either."

Junie smiled at her father, and then she leaned back with a contented look on her face. Kylie knew the picture they represented to their daughter. A family.

For the first time in years, Junie had both of her parents together. What little girl didn't want to sit between her parents, believing her family could be whole?

The truck bounced along the paved road between Wagoner and Sunset Ridge. They were going east, and the sun, sinking now into the western horizon, was behind them. The orange glow settled over the interior of the truck.

"I really could stay at my own place and take care of myself."

Next to her, Junie let out a squeak, but then clamped her lips tight.

Mark gave her a too-cheerful look. "Doctor's orders, Kylie."

"I know," she muttered, not feeling as thankful for

his help as she probably should feel. "All of this fuss over an appendectomy."

"It's just for a few days," he assured her. "And it was a bit more than your run-of-the-mill appendectomy."

"I'm better," Kylie argued.

"Yes, you are." He kept driving, and the conversation lagged.

Next to her, Junie's head dipped, and then she swayed to the side, coming to rest against Kylie. Her lashes brushed her cheeks, and her lips parted on a light snore. Kylie put an arm around her and drew her closer, content to let the moment be, because moments like this were special.

The drive to the Rocking R took twenty minutes. The scenery was wintery and brown with only spots of green to break up the landscape. There were few houses, just long stretches of land. She knew the drive so well. She'd been on these roads hundreds of times, at his side, in an old pickup truck. In their teen years, she sat next to him, his arm across her leg as he'd reach to shift gears. This truck happened to be an automatic, so no shifting required. And this time, Junie sat between them.

He turned onto the driveway that led to the farmhouse that had been in the Rivers' family for more than a hundred years. In years past, the place had fallen into disrepair. But things were looking up for the Rocking R. The barns had been repaired, the fences were no longer sagging and livestock grazed the fields. Those changes had been brought about by Matthew Rivers, Mark's older brother and the new pastor of Sunset Ridge Community Church, a church that seemed to be busting at the seams since Matthew's arrival.

"Here we are," Mark announced as he pulled up next to the house.

He jumped out and hurried to Kylie's side, not giving her a chance to get out on her own. He reached for her hand, as if she couldn't manage.

"Mark, I'm fine."

"I know," he said with a shy grin, looking a lot like the boy she'd known. "I'm taking care of you."

"I can take care of myself," she said. She sounded rather ungracious, even to her own ears. "I'm sorry. Thank you."

"Let me help you," he said in a softer tone. He didn't mean from the truck to the house. She knew he meant to help her in other ways. The business. Her mother. Junie.

There was a danger in relying on Mark.

She slid from the seat, her feet hitting the ground and her legs going suddenly weak. Junie hurried from the truck, rushing to greet the Australian shepherd that Matthew had given Buck when his old dog had gone over the rainbow bridge. The new dog was Molly, or something like that.

The dog raced around in circles, tucking her tail between her legs when Mark commanded her to "settle down, Molly." Junie, like the dog, immediately went still.

Yep, Molly.

"I don't want the dog to bump into you," Mark told her as he reached for the overnight bag in the back of the truck.

"Mark," Kylie warned in a controlled whisper. "I'm fine. Don't scare your daughter or that dog."

He helped her up the steps to the wide front porch of the two-story farmhouse. "I'm not scaring anyone."

Junie and the dog were, again, racing around the yard.

"Do they look scared?" he asked.

"No, they don't." But she was afraid. Frightened

by how good it felt to have him near, to lean on his strength, to feel protected by him.

She'd been strong for a very long time. Today she wanted to be a little weak, to lean on someone. It was just rotten circumstances that he happened to be that someone.

Maybe they needed this time together, to heal and to let go of the past, to forgive? When he left again, they'd be in a better place and more able to trust each other. The thought seemed logical and ridiculous all at the same time.

From the porch, Kylie turned to watch Junie with the dog. She tossed a stick, and the dog chased after it, not bringing it back. Junie giggled and called to the animal to bring it over. She said it in a loud, firm voice that the dog ignored.

Junie needed a pet. A dog, a cat, maybe a bunny. A pet, in Kylie's mind, meant messes. Pets could quickly get out of control. One pet led to two, or six. She shuddered at the thought. Her daughter needed an animal, but Kylie didn't know if she could let go of her memories in order to supply the need.

The front door opened, and Buck stood there, once a towering figure, now stooped with age and hard living. He motioned them inside.

"Get on in here. I've got dinner cooking, and I've made you up the spare room downstairs. Less walking that way." He patted her shoulder with a gnarled but still strong hand.

"Thank you, Buck. I'm sorry for imposing."

"Kylie, you're family. Now come on in and take a load off." Buck's way of telling her to have a seat. She would take him up on that.

The aroma of dinner cooking greeted them as they

entered the large, immaculate country kitchen. Mark pulled out a chair at the table, and she sat down. Junie had followed them inside, the dog panting next to her.

"Junie, the dog should be outside." Kylie motioned toward the door.

"No, she lives in here." Junie gave the dog an affectionate pat on the head. "Doesn't she, Grandpa Buck?"

"She does indeed spend part of her time here with us. Don't worry, she's a good little gal and doesn't make messes." Buck had already moved to the stove, where he stirred whatever he'd left cooking there. "I hope you don't mind homemade chicken and dumplings. I wanted something easy on your system and nutritious."

"It sounds wonderful after several days of hospital food, and it smells even better." Kylie didn't mind saying so. Her mouth watered at the delightful aromas that filled the kitchen. "I'd forgotten what a cook you are. I should have known, since you always bring something mouthwatering to our church meals."

"It's nothing fancy, but it keeps me out of trouble, and I enjoy it." Buck didn't have to elaborate. She knew he'd worked on sobriety the past couple of years. She glanced from father to son and noticed the dry expression on Mark's face. He didn't like the unspoken comparison or the reminder.

"Let me help you get this on the table." Mark didn't wait and started to move dishes to the table. "Junie, do you want to fill glasses with ice?"

Kylie watched as their daughter hurried to do as he asked.

It all felt very domestic, as if they did this every day.

They were sitting down to eat when they heard the front door close. The dog jumped up from her mat on the floor and ran to greet whoever had entered the house.

"Anyone home?" Matthew called out. His bootsteps on the hardwood followed the greeting.

"We're sitting down like civilized folk and having a meal," Buck called out in a growly and not-so-civilized voice.

Junie giggled, and Kylie shot her a warning look. Unfortunately, Buck gave his granddaughter a quick wink and brought on another burst of laughter.

Matthew entered the room, pulling off his cowboy hat as he did. He looked the image of an Oklahoma rancher, tall and lean, wearing blue jeans, a flannel jacket and dusty boots. This Oklahoma rancher happened to have a dark-haired little girl sleeping against his chest.

"What has you stomping around like an angry bear after a long nap?" Buck asked.

"I'm not stomping. I'm a big guy, and I sound loud, but I just got a call from our worship leader. He's leaving Sunset Ridge. His dad is having health issues, and he needs to be closer to his parent." Matthew's tone rumbled, but he'd lowered the volume so as not to wake his daughter. "How long did you say you're staying?"

Mark shook his head. "Don't look at me. I'll be leaving sooner than later. I have some meetings coming up."

"It was worth a shot." Matthew pulled out a chair and sat down, his hand cradling the back of Faith's head to keep her from being jostled.

"We both know that I'm not in a place to do that job."

Buck had ignored the two of them. He grabbed a bowl, filled it with chicken and dumplings and sat it before Junie. He filled the next bowl and placed it in front of Kylie.

"Grab you one of those hot rolls," he told her as he

moved on to the next bowl. "You boys quit your arguing, and Matthew say grace."

Kylie quickly bowed her head. She listened to Matthew's prayer for the food they were about to receive, and she added her own prayer that Mark's departure wouldn't break their daughter's heart.

After saying "amen," Matthew returned to the conversation. Kylie wanted to tell him to just let it go, but how desperate would that sound?

"I heard you're helping with the Valentine's event in town," Matthew said between bites.

Kylie nearly choked on a bite of roll. "You're doing what?"

Mark's cheeks flushed a deep red, and he cleared his throat. "I just offered a few ideas and some assistance in pulling it all together."

"How did this happen?" she asked.

"The committee ladies came into the coffee shop. They were in a pinch without you there to guide them. It isn't a lot. I'm going to help them set up the music, find a band and arrange for tables to be delivered to the old bank. You know, that place would make a nice venue if someone had the money and time to buy it and fix it up. No reason it should sit empty."

"I've considered it," Kylie admitted. "I haven't wanted to take on more than I could handle."

"Maybe if we find you some decent help?" he suggested as the others listened.

She didn't comment; instead she told herself that he wanted to help and probably didn't see it as interfering. He'd put the sign up to make sure she had someone to take part of the load when he left.

He was temporary.

They were used to living life without him in it.

* * *

Mark knew when to let a topic go. He hadn't always known, but in the past year, he'd gained some skills that had been sadly lacking for most of his life. Letting things go happened to be one of the new skills.

With that in mind, he changed the subject.

"Where did you say your wife was tonight?" Mark asked his brother.

Matthew had a silly grin on his face, the grin he always wore when Parker or their daughter, Faith, was mentioned. "Parker's working the evening shift. I came over to doctor a mare that got cut on barbed wire she found out in the field and to make sure our new foal is doing okay."

Family. Matthew had been given a beautiful family. He'd married his best friend, and they'd adopted Faith. Sometimes things worked out for a person. Things had definitely worked out for Matthew and Parker.

For other people, the path took a few rocky turns. Mark couldn't blame anyone but himself for the loss of his family and his marriage. Moments like this, his mind tricked him. It felt as if they were still whole. But they weren't whole, and Kylie was no longer his. She hadn't been his for a very long time. He couldn't walk back into his wife's and daughter's lives and take claim of them. He couldn't be a temporary father, a temporary husband.

"Need some help in the barn?" Mark asked his older brother as they finished clearing the table.

Kylie sat with Junie, going over the schoolwork their daughter had done that week. Their heads were close, one dark and curly, the other a shimmering silver with a touch of lavender. Her hair was straight and hung to the middle of her back. He had always loved her hair.

"I'd take some help," Matthew said as he put plates in the dishwasher. "Dad, thank you for dinner. That was a lot better than the bologna sandwich I planned to have later."

"You know I always make plenty," Buck grumbled.

Mark chuckled at the growl in their father's voice. Buck might sound half mad, but there was an emotional edge to his tone. He liked having them home. The past five days had proven that to Mark. This house felt more like a home now than ever before.

"Daddy?" Junie's voice caught his attention. It caught his heart.

He had forgotten how that word felt. This past week, he'd heard it more than he had in the three previous years put together.

Matthew caught his eye and winked.

"Yes?" He had to clear his throat to get the simple word to come out.

"Can I go to the barn with you?"

"Of course you can come with me." He said it, and then he wondered if he should have given the answer more thought. He'd been playing at being her father for the past five days, but he still had a lot of catching up to do.

He had trust to earn back.

"If it's okay with your mom," he added a few seconds too late.

"We'll both go," Kylie said with ease.

"Should you?"

She sighed. "I need fresh air, Mark. I've been stuck inside for days. I need to be outside, and the barn always makes me happy."

"We can all go," Matthew interjected. "If I'm going

to doctor that mare, it would help to have someone there to hold Faith."

Matthew smiled down at his daughter. She'd woken up, and she yawned loudly, reaching to touch his cheek. Mark felt an uncomfortable pain, something that had to be envy. Matthew had walked away from a church that had made him somewhat famous. He'd even written books about faith, about grief, about finding himself all over again.

And yet the smile on his face had nothing to do with anything he'd accomplished in life. His greatest accomplishment had dark eyes and dark hair and dimples in her cheeks.

"I'm going to rest for a bit," Buck announced. "You boys can take care of the farm work."

"Thank you for dinner, Cookie," Matthew said as he gave Buck a quick hug. "I'll probably head home after I take care of the livestock. I'll see you tomorrow."

"Maybe we can go to Chuck's for breakfast?" Buck said.

"We might just do that."

As the four of them, plus baby Faith, headed to the barn, Mark drew in a deep breath of country air. It was warm for January but still cool. The air was damp, and the clouds were low and heavy in the night sky. Maybe it would rain. Hopefully, it wouldn't snow.

"The place looks good," Mark told his brother.

"You've contributed."

Money, the thing he always had to give. Time and labor would have been appreciated, he guessed. He'd never enjoyed visits to the ranch he'd grown up hating. He'd wanted as far away from the place as possible. For most of his life, that had been his goal.

When it came down to it, maybe he wasn't so different from their mother. He didn't like to think about Izzy. Thoughts of her always brought a painful wave of guilt. His nine-year-old self had been the reason she left. Or at least the catalyst for her departure. He'd left her chickens out, and a fox or coyote had gotten hold of them. Izzy had told him he was as worthless as his drunken father and she was done with the lot of them.

Those words had stayed with him his whole life.

He'd only told one person, other than his therapist, about the pain those words caused, the scars they'd left. Kylie knew. Only Kylie. Just as he knew her secrets.

Matthew pushed open the wide doors to the barn and flipped on a light.

"This makes the old barn look pretty sad and decrepit," Mark said after a long whistle of appreciation.

"I hated tearing down the old barn, but with the money it was going to take to keep doing repairs, it made sense to rebuild. I built Parker a chicken coop out of the old barnwood. I wanted something of the place to remain."

"You're awfully sentimental," Mark said with more humor in his voice than he felt.

"Yeah, I guess I am." Matthew pulled Faith out of the pouch. "Kylie, are you sure you can wrangle her? She's mighty squirmy these days."

"I'll sit on the bench, and she can sit with us. Junie can help keep her entertained."

"Do I have…" Junie faltered, probably due to the look her mother sent her. "I mean, I'd love to play with Faith."

"I promise if you help me for a few minutes, you can also help your uncle Matthew and your daddy with the horses." Kylie patted the bench, and Junie clambered up next to her, opening her arms to hold Faith.

Mark felt the embarrassing sting of tears as he watched his ex-wife and daughter snuggle together with Faith between them. He blinked away the dampness and found a smile.

"Do you need anything?"

Kylie looked up, her eyes brilliant and her face so at peace. Being in her presence loosened something inside of him, something tightly coiled and tense. He hadn't even realized he'd been that way until being around her undid it all.

"We're good," she assured him. "It's fun to sit and get baby snuggles and Junie snuggles, too. I've missed my girl."

"She missed you," he said. "I'm not too good at reading princess bedtime stories."

"You coming?" Matthew had entered a storage room, and he now held a bucket with supplies and another bucket of grain.

"Lead the way."

Matthew led him to the last stall. Inside, a pretty mare, deep bay with a white blaze down her dainty face, snuffled at hay and then brushed her muzzle through the water, blowing lightly.

"Pretty horse," Mark said as he entered the stall right behind his older brother. "You have some nice animals."

"I'm doing my best to build the place up. We owe our kids a legacy and not a rundown money pit with taxes due and fences falling over."

"I agree. Have you hired help?"

He thought about Junie, growing up in Sunset Ridge, perhaps someday having her own place on this ranch. A grown-up Junie with a solid and respectable life that included a good husband and pretty babies.

"I have a couple of guys that I call when I need

them. You could always stay," Matthew said after a few minutes.

Mark held the mare's halter and soothed her with whispers and a light hand on her neck. His brother applied a salve to the numerous cuts that wrapped around her slender fetlock.

"She did a number on herself," Mark said, needing to move away from the topic of his staying. He needed to go, to get away from the tangled-up feelings that came with spending time in the presence of his wife—no, ex-wife—and daughter.

Matthew looked up, a searching expression on his face before he shook his head.

"Yeah, rain always manages to uncover old barbed-wire fences. She found this section somewhere by the east pond. Fortunately for her, I was out searching for a cow that I knew was about to calf. Smart little filly, she didn't fight the wire. She stood there, waiting for someone to come rescue her. She was trembling and about to fall down, but she never panicked."

"Would she make a good horse for a little girl?" Mark wondered aloud.

Matthew finished with the sticky salve, wiped his hands on a cloth and shrugged. The two of them had often been mistaken for twins. They both had the silver-gray eyes of their father and his thick, dark hair. Matthew kept his short. Mark preferred his a little longer. Or maybe his publicist preferred his hair a little longer. He could no longer remember what he really liked or didn't.

"She needs a little time under the saddle, but by the time that little girl is ready for a good horse, this one will be waiting for her. I'll make sure she's well-trained."

"Thank you."

"Or you could stay…"

Mark shook his head at the suggestion. "They're better off without me."

"Are they?" Matthew asked. He soothed the filly, rubbing his hand across her withers. "Charity. That's her name."

"Who named her that?"

"My wife." Matthew said it with a thread of warning.

"Good choice." Mark grinned. "I probably would have picked that name, too."

"You would have named her something like Renegade or Goober. I think you had a horse named Goober."

"I did, and he was."

"And yet you poke fun at Charity. Faith, Hope and Charity."

"When will you have a Hope?" Mark asked, now curious about the gleam in his brother's eyes.

"Now that, little brother, is something we haven't announced. How did you know?"

"You're glowing," Mark teased.

"We're adopting a little girl," Matthew admitted. "She's due in about six weeks."

Mark slapped his brother on the back, causing the horse, Charity, to dance a little. "Congratulations."

"What are congratulations?" Junie asked, peering over the top of the stall door.

"Hey, how did you get so tall?" Mark asked his daughter.

She giggled. "I have a stool, silly. Isn't Charity a pretty horse, Daddy?"

"She is indeed. I was telling your uncle Matthew congratulations for having such a nice horse."

"Faith is hungry."

"I'll finish feeding the horse if you want to take Faith

to the house," Mark offered to his brother. "Maybe Junie can head on back with you?"

"What about Mommy?" Junie asked.

"I'll walk her back." Mark didn't know why he'd made the suggestion. Maybe the subject of babies had him sentimental? Maybe it was the January night and the full moon. The last thing he needed was time alone with Kylie. But at the moment, he wanted that time more than anything he'd ever wanted in his life.

Chapter Six

Kylie sat on the bench, feeling a little bit helpless as Matthew bundled up his daughter and took her daughter by the hand. She didn't like feeling this way, and it had happened too often in the past five days. Mark had a way of taking over.

"Why did you do that?" she asked as the door closed behind Matthew and Junie.

Mark sat down next to her. They were shoulder to shoulder, so close she could smell the horse scent combined with his cologne, a fragrance he'd always used. It was something wild and beautiful, like a walk through a pine forest to a mountain lake.

He shrugged. "Selfish, I guess. You should be used to that."

"Stop," she shushed him.

"You think I'm not?" He bumped against her, smiling down with a wolfish grin.

"Oh, I know you can be. I also know that you can be kind and giving, protective and…" She didn't want this conversation. It brought back memories of the boy she'd loved, before he self-destructed.

"I don't like it when you take over. Please, next time

ask me my opinion on the decisions you make concerning me."

He nodded in agreement. "I can do that."

And then they were silent.

The soothing sounds of the barn surrounded them like a cocoon. Horses stomping, snuffling in their hay, overhead the soft tread of a barn cat running through the loft. It smelled of dust, hay and animals.

The air got cooler. Kylie shivered, and he drew her close to his side, wrapping an arm around her and holding her in a gentle embrace.

"I need to apologize," he said after a few minutes. "That's why I came back. Not to disrupt your life, but to tell you how sorry I am. If you could forgive me. Maybe not today, but someday."

"I've forgiven you," she assured him. "Have you forgiven yourself?"

"I'm working on that. I just need to make sure you are okay, and Junie."

"We're okay." She said it simply; it was what he needed to know. "We're happy in Sunset Ridge. We have our friends and our church. I have my business."

"I'm glad," he said softly. Maybe wistfully?

"So that's why you came to see us, to make amends."

"Steps eight, nine and ten. The rest have been finding my way back to God and my faith. But these three steps are important. You forgiving me is important. And step ten. When I'm wrong, I have to admit it. I think that's a hard one for me because I have to let go of that stubborn Rivers pride. I can't come into your life at this late juncture and take over. You were right to be angry. I was wrong to think I had the right to be in charge."

"This means a lot to me," she told him. "And I'm glad you can see a way forward. I'm glad you're doing better."

"Me, too. The last time I was here, I definitely wasn't my best self." He scrubbed a hand over his face. "I'm not sure if I've ever been my best self, but I'm working on it. For Junie. I guess for you, too."

"Mark…" How did she tell him that he didn't owe her?

"I know, there is no us, and you're not exactly waiting for me or wanting anything more from me. I didn't come here to complicate your life, Kylie. I know that you are better off without me."

She reached for his hand, lacing her fingers through his. It was a dangerous move, but he needed comforting, and she could give him that. She could also lighten the moment.

"About that last time you were here. Wow, you made an impact on some people."

He chuckled. "Yeah, not the best moment in my life. I sang Garth Brooks and fell through the doors of the church. Or so I've been told by my stalwart brother, Luke. I owe him."

"He made a decision that day to get you sober and to save your life." She removed her hand from his. It felt too much like the past, having his hand in hers. "I'm glad he did."

"Same. Do you think maybe someday we could be friends again? I've missed having my best friend."

"I think we can work on friendship. I think Junie needs for us to be friends. She needs you in her life. If we're grown-ups together, her life will be better for it."

"Could I visit?"

"You can visit Junie." She sighed. "I'm not quite ready to send her off with you."

"Wise woman," he agreed. "Let's go to the house. This has been a long outing for you."

"I am tired," she admitted.

Kylie allowed him to pull her to her feet. They left the barn, turning out the lights and closing the door behind them. The sky was midnight blue with a sprinkling of stars. They walked back to the house in the dark, in silence. Mark kept an arm around her, a protective arm.

She wanted to move away, but her heart told her to stay, just for the time being. She lied to herself, saying she needed his strength. She'd had surgery, after all.

When he stopped walking, she didn't protest. When he cupped her cheek with a warm, strong hand, she didn't tell him no. There was a full moon and brilliant, sparkling stars now that the clouds had drifted away. The January air had grown cold, and somewhere in the distance, a coyote howled. Memories were dangerous things. They drew a person in and reminded them of what they missed, reminded them of the good times. In a rearview mirror, everything looked distorted, different.

Mark lowered his head, capturing her mouth in a kiss that made her think of their teen years and being in love. It was a love he'd misused. He'd wounded her, leaving scars that made love seem like a cheap gift, something disposable to be tossed away.

For a moment, she forgot the heartache. For a moment, it was just the two of them again. Two kids from Sunset Ridge, seeking a better life, the promise of forever, of being cared for and cherished. His mouth cherished hers.

The heartache of being left resurfaced, bringing with it a healthy dose of common sense.

"No," she told him. "I'm not doing this. We can only work on friendship if you don't do that again. I need boundaries."

He closed his eyes, nodding slowly. "You're right. Blame it on the moonlight."

"Or the past," she quipped.

"You're my most treasured childhood memory. I'm sorry that I didn't treasure you as the gift you were meant to be."

"No, you didn't treasure me." She put a hand to his cheek to soften the words. "I'll never allow Junie to grow up the way I grew up."

He whistled softly. "So that's how you see me?"

She nodded, a tear slipping free to trickle down her cheek. "You're chaos. I won't have her growing up never knowing which Mark will show up. Right now, you're the sober, attentive man that I knew. Tomorrow..."

"I might fall back into the bottle. I know that, and that's why I'm determined to let you be. The two of you deserve the best, and if I can't be the best, then I can't be in your lives."

"You have to be in her life, Mark. For her, be your best self."

His thumb traced the path of the tear that had broken free. In his expression, she saw that he understood. What they'd been, they could never again be.

Mark woke up early Saturday morning. So early the sun hadn't even broken the eastern horizon. The rooster crowed, and in the distance the cattle mooed, probably following a farm truck toward their morning grain.

He'd been sober—he looked at his watch—387 days. Not one drink. In over a year. There were times, like last night, that he wondered why he even cared to be sober. He couldn't have his wife. He could only have visits with his daughter. Three hundred eighty-seven days of clear thinking, rotten memories that couldn't be forgotten and loneliness.

Last night, he'd considered searching the kitchen cabinets for a bottle. He hadn't. He'd prayed. He'd reminded himself why he had taken this journey for the past year.

Sobriety was more than clear thinking and loneliness. It meant fewer embarrassing moments and not hurting the people he cared about. Sobriety meant living longer, watching his daughter grow up, maybe someday being a grandfather.

Last night, his dad had caught him sitting in the kitchen, talking himself into staying sober. It had been the hardest night in six months. He should have known better than to kiss Kylie. He needed to remember that his place in her life could be as a helper, not as a husband. Their marriage had ended, and now they were in a new stage, friendship.

Buck had prayed with him last night. It had possibly been the strongest father-son moment in their lives. It was a memory that would replace some of the fuzzier or harder ones.

He hit his knees again, needing the solitude of early morning prayer time. He had verses that he kept in his mind for moments such as this. He had the prayer that he knew he could always say when things got tough.

"God grant me the serenity to accept the things I cannot change and the courage to change the things I can."

The house was silent when he left for town. Buck might have been up and in the barns, but Mark didn't go searching for him. He drove to Sunset Ridge and parked in the square, just down from the coffee shop. There were lights on in Chuck's Café, which meant Chuck and Jenni were hard at it, getting ready for their breakfast crowd. Their place would fill up with the regulars, the farmers, the town business folks, the retirees. The coffee shop had a different clientele. Mostly, it seemed to serve the people on their way to work in towns other than Sunset Ridge, and it served the local ladies who wanted to gather in groups.

Mark unlocked the door of the coffee shop and switched on the lights. He started the coffeemaker; it had some type of heating-up function. He didn't know what he'd serve, but he knew what he was craving for his own breakfast. Grilled PB and J. Buttered bread and inside, creamy peanut butter and raspberry jam. It was too sweet and not exactly the best way to start a day, but it sure did taste good with a cup of coffee.

He'd just gotten his sandwich off the griddle when the door opened. A woman close to his age, probably a little younger, entered. She had short blond hair and a dimpled smile.

"Mark Rivers! I never thought I'd see you in here." She reached back to open the door. "I brought my dad in for breakfast. I didn't realize Kylie wouldn't be here."

"She's been sick." He probably narrowed his eyes as he studied her, trying to place her. She noticed and flashed those dimples again. She wasn't flirting, just friendly. She looked sweet, the kind of young woman that everyone liked.

"I hope she's better soon," she said.

He made a noise, and she gave him another amused look.

"Jennifer Bryers. I was a few years younger than you in school and not as cool."

Bryers? Ah, yes, pretty girl with dimples and far too innocent for any of the Rivers boys. And yet...

"Right, I remember. Did you date my brother Jonah?"

She turned a bright shade of pink. "Not really. We pretended to date."

"Oh." He'd been right, too innocent for the Rivers brothers. The brief flash of pain in her eyes said it had been important. To her. Jonah had never been good at relationships and still wasn't. Of course, the Rivers brothers didn't have the best role models. "I'm sorry if he hurt you."

It wasn't his apology to make, but it seemed that something needed to be said.

"I obviously survived." She reached to help the older gentleman to a table. Too old to be a father, or so he thought. He tried to remember what he'd known about Jennifer and realized it wasn't much.

"Do you have quiche or breakfast sandwiches?"

"Not yet. I'm going to work on that this afternoon. Cooking isn't my best skill."

"Whatever you have, it smells good." That came from the elderly Mr. Bryers.

"I made myself a grilled PB and J," he admitted as he showed them the plate.

"Is that on the menu?" Jennifer asked.

"I guess it is now."

"We'll take two and two regular coffees. The Kenyan blend if you have it."

"I'll see what I can find."

A few minutes later, he had coffee made. He'd found a big thermal carafe, and he filled it, hoping to serve it to customers if it stayed hot.

He carried two cups out to Jennifer and Mr. Bryers, and then he finished up their sandwiches and delivered those to the table. The door opened to three more customers. He greeted them and headed back to the counter. And so it went for the rest of the morning. Coffee, grilled PB and J, plus the occasional bagel and smoked salmon that he'd found in the freezer and thawed.

The door opened again. This time the customers were his father, his daughter and Kylie. Kylie glanced around the crowded dining area and made a face.

"What are you feeding people?" she whispered.

"Grilled PB and J," he said with a wink.

She put a hand to her forehead in a more dramatic fashion than was typical of Kylie. "You'll ruin me."

"Everyone looks pretty happy to me. I even learned to make a latte. The internet has videos for everything, even this crazy complicated coffeemaker. Now, if you don't mind, I have cupcakes in the oven."

"Cupcakes?"

"Yes, cupcakes. This coffee shop business is a breeze. A guy just needs the internet and some imagination."

"Uh-oh," his daughter whispered to her grandfather. No, not really a whisper, more a stage whisper followed by a definite giggle.

"What's going on?" Buck sniffed as he asked and leaned to look in the kitchen. "I don't smell anything burning. As a matter of fact, I'm going to have one of whatever he's cooking in there."

Kylie ignored them. She greeted a few of her customers and then made her way to the kitchen. Mark watched her go, amused by the worried pucker of her brow. She had nothing to worry about. It really hadn't been all that difficult to throw together some cupcakes. A few eggs, some flour and sugar, mix the ingredients and presto, cupcakes.

He'd enjoyed the process of creating. Maybe baking would be his new hobby.

"What have you done to my kitchen!" Her voice rose to a volume that made every head turn.

"Uh-oh, again," Junie said as she hurried around the counter to see what had her mother so upset. She glanced back at her grandfather. "Have a seat, Grandpa Buck, this might take a hot minute."

"Hot minute?" Kylie said, releasing a breath between slightly clenched teeth.

Mark's hopes and dreams of winning a television reality show for his new baking skills evaporated. He stood in the doorway of the kitchen, Junie tucking herself under his arm to peer inside.

"Uh…" Junie started.

"Don't." Kylie raised a hand to stop the third *uh-oh* in five minutes. Her kitchen had been forgotten. He thought he had a reprieve, but then realized that wasn't the case. "Where did you get that slang?"

"It's my fault," Mark admitted. "Slang not allowed. I'll do better." And he meant it.

"That obviously isn't the worst thing she could say, but…" She closed her eyes just briefly. "It's fine. My kitchen isn't."

"I'm going to be a better man. And I'll clean up my mess."

The latter he said only for her ears, leaning in close. Close enough to feel the silkiness of that silvery hair brushing against his face, to smell the herbal scent of her shampoo. He'd never stopped loving her. He'd just been really bad at loving her the way she deserved.

What did it mean, he wondered, when the Bible said to love a wife the way Christ loved the church? He needed to do some research on that because he'd obviously fallen short.

"I know," she said softly, her expression matching her tone. She quickly drew herself together, obviously remembering last night and her conviction to not get tangled up in their past.

He had the same thoughts. He wouldn't go there. The last thing he wanted to do was hurt them. The easiest way to keep that from happening was to keep the boundaries between them.

"Back to my kitchen!" She shook her head as she surveyed the mess.

"I might not be the neatest cook, but I know these cupcakes will be amazing."

"But what happened!" She'd always needed her world neat and tidy. It came from living with her mother, Mindy. He hadn't expected her to show up and see the mess. From her perspective, he guessed it looked pretty bad.

"The flour exploded, and I broke an egg."

"The flour more than exploded. This is a disaster." She grabbed a broom, but he took it from her.

"You're not allowed to clean," he reminded. "You're resting. I'm taking care of business."

"You're going to ruin my business."

"I tried to hire someone," he informed her. "One girl applied, and I didn't feel comfortable with the situation."

"Young?"

"Yes, and maybe infatuated."

"Well, you are cute." She closed her eyes and bit down on her bottom lip. "I didn't say that."

"No take backs," he said. "You're pretty cute yourself."

She walked away from him, swiping her hand over the flour-covered countertops. "Stop being charming and funny or this won't work."

"Got it, no funny or charming. I'll scowl and look unkempt."

"You could cut your hair," she suggested.

"Not happening." He swept up the floor while she wiped down the counters.

"One thing you have to learn is that when you bake, it's easier to clean as you go."

"Taking notes," he promised.

"Good," she said, and then her face scrunched up a little. She reached for the counter.

He hurried to her side and wrapped an arm around her too-thin waist. "Sit down."

"It was just a twinge."

He didn't buy that. "You have to rest. I've got this."

"I know you do." She looked around the kitchen. "Kind of. It's just, I need to get back on my feet before you have to leave because I'm sure you didn't intend to come here and play chef, or nursemaid."

"I'm up to the challenge."

"The longer you stay, the harder this is going to be. We can't pretend we're okay, or that we're the kids we used to be. Too much has happened."

"Okay." He had no choice but to agree with her. He had appointments in Nashville. She had good reasons for keeping the walls between them. "Then let's get the word out so we can find someone to help you."

"I will. I have a couple of women from church that I can call." She stood to get herself a bottle of water. He worried that the minute he wasn't watching, she'd overdo it.

The timer on the stove went off. He hurried to take the cupcakes out, praying they wouldn't be burnt and that she might be a little impressed.

"I don't serve cupcakes," she told him as he put the pan on the top of the stove.

"Well, this week you might have to because there's nothing else, except my special sandwich."

She wrinkled her nose at his creation.

"They're only a little brown," he defended.

"They're vanilla, right?"

"Yes, they are, but…" He laughed as she pried a cupcake from the pan. "This is why you have to hire someone. You can't have a coffee shop where your menu consists of burnt cupcakes and grilled sandwiches. In my defense, I followed the directions, even on the time they were supposed to be in the oven."

"I rarely follow those directions. I set the timer for five minutes sooner, sometimes ten, check the product and reset the timer accordingly."

"According to what?"

"To how done they are. Like these cupcakes. For these, I would have set the timer for fifteen minutes. The recipe probably said twenty or twenty-five."

"You are correct."

"When they're done, cupcakes and cakes bounce back when you touch them. So do pancakes."

"Got it, bounce back. Or the toothpick method?"

"Or that." She surveyed the brown cupcakes. "No worries, I'm going to stick around. Junie wanted to spend time with you, and she should."

He liked that idea, of Junie and Kylie hanging out with him. For most of Junie's life, he'd been an absent father, a statistic of the modern age. He hadn't read bedtime stories or said her prayers with her. He hadn't taken her to the princess dances or to gymnastics lessons. He hadn't done any of the stuff that mattered; he'd just sent the checks that paid for it.

Princess dances. The thought came to him with an idea because, just once, he should be here for the dance, to escort his daughter. He needed to be more present in her life. He could help create something that would make every little girl in town feel like a princess, including Junie. And he could be here to escort her, as a father should.

If he helped organize Valentine's Day in Sunset Ridge, as well as a princess ball for younger attendees, he'd have to spend time in Sunset Ridge. He'd have to spend time with Junie, and with Kylie. That meant he'd be back in a matter of weeks. He started thinking about the things he needed to take care of in Nashville, appointments that had already been set up. As fast as his thoughts went in that direction, he yanked them to a halt. Making amends meant doing things better, not just asking for forgiveness. If he played the game that way, he'd always be asking for forgiveness.

He needed to be present in his own life and his daughter's life.

For the past dozen years, he'd been selfishly drowning himself in booze and chasing a career that he thought made him somebody. He hadn't realized that the most important person he could be was the person Junie called Daddy. He should have been the most important person to Kylie, the husband she deserved. He'd lost that opportunity, but he still had a chance with Junie.

He guessed there was a song in there, somewhere. A song about the important things in life and the mistake of chasing after the wrong things. He would never love another, but he wasn't good enough for the one he loved.

"Hey, I could use some help out here." Buck stepped into the kitchen. "And there's a lady asking to talk to you about a kitten you wanted."

"I'll be right out." He avoided looking at Kylie. He hadn't expected the kitten to show up here.

Kylie gave him a sharp look and started to say something. He hurried from the kitchen to avoid having to explain.

In retrospect, the kitten might have been a mistake. A man making amends didn't want to just keep adding things to the list that he needed to apologize for.

Chapter Seven

Kylie made the decision to go home Saturday evening. It had been over a week since the surgery. Her follow up appointment had gone well, and she felt much better. She could manage on her own. She wanted her house, her bed, her comfy chair. She wanted her space. It had taken a bit to convince Mark, but she'd finally helped him to see that they needed to get back to their own lives.

When they pulled to her front door, her heart exhaled. Everything inside her relaxed. For the first time in days, she felt peace. She was home. She loved the grand old house with its curving staircase to the second floor, the high ceilings of the foyer, the dining room with floor-to-ceiling windows that overlooked the park-like backyard. The house had dignity, something her life had been sadly missing for so many years.

It was borrowed dignity; she knew that. She'd bought this home, needing a place to call her own, even though it had belonged to people she envied and resented. A little part of her had thought that maybe owning this house would make her better, more acceptable…a part of their lives.

She tried to picture a cat in her peaceful world.

Cats looked dignified, but they weren't. Cats meowed in a way that sounded like the feline equivalent of howling. They also ransacked the house, shredded furniture and carpets, and they were picky.

"You okay?" Mark asked as he took his keys from the ignition of the truck.

They couldn't have this conversation. He noticed the direction of her gaze and so did Junie. She sat between her parents, the cat carrier in her lap. They'd picked the animal up after leaving the ranch. Her first inclination had been to tell Mark to keep the cat, but she'd caved because the kitten was important to her daughter.

Junie gave her a cheerful look, cheeks dimpling. "I promise to take care of her."

"I know you will," Kylie said, and the delighted look on her daughter's face made her decision concerning the kitten a little easier.

Once upon a time, before her mother started hoarding animals, Kylie had loved kittens, too. Junie shouldn't have to pay the price for Kylie's own childhood trauma. It wasn't fair. She'd given herself that pep talk at the coffee shop when she learned that Mark had arranged for their daughter to have the animal.

"Let's go inside," she said as she pushed the door open. "I feel like we've been gone forever."

"We were…" Junie started, but then she clamped her mouth shut.

"You were what?" Kylie asked.

"We were going to…" Junie looked from her mother to her father. "I thought we were staying longer with Grandpa Buck and my dad."

Kylie had a distinct feeling that Junie had wanted to say something more than that.

"I'm sure Grandpa Buck will be glad to get his house back. And your father is leaving. We already discussed that."

"But I'll be back," he quickly added.

Junie started to pout, but she pulled herself together. Her liquid gaze focused on her father. "I liked doing school and baking with you."

"I loved it more than anything in life," Mark answered.

Kylie could see that he meant it. He'd been gone for so long, and now that he had bounced back into their lives, she wanted him to be this person for Junie. She wanted him to show up and to do the little things, as well as the big.

He carried her suitcase up the front steps and waited as she unlocked the door. The cat cried from inside the carrier, and Junie hopped around impatiently. It gave her more than a little thrill to know that Junie had a home she loved, a life she loved. Kylie had done what she set out to do: she'd given her child happiness and stability.

She pushed the door open, and they entered. Her senses were assaulted by the smell of cleaning supplies and flowers. She stepped a little farther into the house. Everything gleamed. She dropped her keys, and Mark stooped to pick them up for her.

There were flowers. So many flowers. She started laughing, and she laughed until she cried. "What in the world?"

"We surprised you!" Junie jumped around, jostling the cat carrier. The feline inside gave a startled yowl.

"You definitely surprised me. I didn't expect this."

"It's okay?" Mark asked, looking unsure of himself.

"It's definitely okay. You did this?"

"I hired a cleaning crew that Parker recommended.

I would have done it myself, but it wouldn't have been this clean."

"It doesn't matter," Kylie assured him. "I love it."

"Let's get you comfortable," he said as his hand went to the small of her back. "Living room?"

"My sitting room. That's where we spend most of our time. The room has magnificent windows." She'd picked furniture in pastel colors and wall hangings in floral prints. Everything in the room spoke of comfort. It was welcoming and warm.

"You've always loved this old house," Mark said as she led him through the house to the room in question.

"I had an unhealthy obsession with this house," she corrected.

"Because of who he was."

They didn't say his name or discuss it. They both knew what she'd thought about the family that lived in this house, the father that lived here, giving his children everything while she had nothing. That man was the reason her mother had dragged them to Sunset Ridge, probably hoping he'd do something more for them than buy the rundown trailer.

"Can I take my kitten upstairs to my room?" Junie asked.

"Yes, but don't forget that he has a litterbox and litter in the truck that need to be set up before he has an accident. You have to take care of him. Fill up his water bowl and give him food."

"I will, Mommy. I love you." Junie gave Kylie a quick hug, then she turned to Mark, and the hug she gave held on a little longer. Kylie feared for her daughter, for her tender heart that loved her daddy so much.

Her own heart had been trampled by him.

"I have a healthier attitude these days," she informed

him as they entered the sitting room. "I went to him. It was two years ago. He and his wife live in Tulsa. I drove up there by myself, and I told him what I thought and how I felt about him."

"What did he say? How did he react?"

"He didn't deny that I'm his daughter. He simply doesn't want anything to do with me. I get that—he doesn't have a bond with me. I'm a stranger."

"He should have wanted to know you. You're remarkable, and he missed out."

"It's okay, really." As she said it, she realized that it had become the truth. She was over it. All of it. She'd given it to God. She'd found healing for her soul.

"Still, I'm sorry," Mark said as he sat on the ottoman.

"Don't be. I told him what I wanted to say and let him know that I bought this house. I told him I forgive him. Surprisingly, that was enough. I needed to tell him that he was my father, and I needed to forgive him."

"You've had to forgive the men in your life who should have been there for you."

"We're living in the present, Mark, not the past. The past holds us in chains and keeps us tied to memories. I need to move forward."

"I agree," he said. "Forward is my only option. Can I get you something before I leave? Or if it would help, I can stay here and sleep on the sofa. You look like this day has taken a lot out of you."

"That isn't a compliment." Her words brought a streak of red to his cheeks, and that amused her. She loved when he got flustered.

She loved it so much, the way she'd always loved him.

"You're always beautiful," he rushed to say, and then he closed his eyes, looking prayerful, thoughtful. When his eyes opened, he'd grown serious, and she knew that he wouldn't be stopped from whatever he planned to say.

"Can we start over?"

"Mark, we ended a long time ago. There's no going back."

He waved his hand around, shaking his head at the same time. "No, that isn't what I mean. I know that I'm not good relationship material. I'm barely able to trust myself."

"Then what do you mean?"

"I miss you. I miss our friendship, the way we used to be. We were there for each other. We had each other's backs. We were good as friends."

"I see." She did, but now that he'd said it, she felt let down, almost hurt. What she should feel, what she needed to feel was relief. He was right, they had been good as friends. Their marriage had destroyed them. His career had torn apart the remnants of their relationship.

"I'd like to be your friend. I want to be here for you. I want time with my daughter."

"Is that what this is all about, Junie? You have had years to be in her life, and you chose to only make brief visits."

"Sobriety has opened my eyes. Being sober literally took away the haze that I'd been living in. I want to be your friend and her father. I want to be a better man for the two of you."

"We can try. But don't hurt us. Don't let us down."

"I'm going to do my very best."

She wanted to believe him, believe in him. She didn't want him to pay for the sins of her mother, but she couldn't help it. Throughout her childhood, Mindy had promised to be better, to do better. During their marriage, Mark had also made the promises.

She would never give him complete trust. He'd had it once, and he'd tossed it away. *Fool me once, shame on you*, went the old saying. *Fool me twice, shame on me.* She wouldn't be his fool.

Mark found his way upstairs and to his daughter's room. As he approached the door, he could hear her singing to the kitten. The song ended, and she began to tell the animal a story about bunny rabbits and insisted the cat understand that bunnies are nice and not to be chased.

As he drew up to her door, the story stopped. "Is that you, Daddy?"

"It's me." He peered inside.

He chuckled at the sight before him. She had managed to get the kitten in a dress, and it was curled up in a toy stroller, a tiny diaper visible beneath the pink outfit.

"What?" Junie asked, her brow furrowing in an imitation of her mother.

"I like the outfit. I think the kitten will prefer this litterbox." He lifted the bags of supplies he'd purchased for the kitten.

"I think I'd rather wear a diaper than put my paws in that," Junie insisted.

"Cats are different. They like to dig."

"Is the cat mends?" She asked the question with a little twist of her mouth and a pucker between her eyes.

"Mends?" He struggled to figure that one out.

"Yes, mends."

He must have looked very confused because she made a face and shook her head at his cluelessness.

"Like you're apologizing again." She picked the kitten up and held it close. "I already forgave you. I don't need mends."

"Amends," he corrected as gently as he could. He felt pummeled, truly knocked down by her words, by her expression. Would everything he did for her be something suspect, as if he could only do kind things as penance for the past?

"Is it?" She was persistent.

"No. The cat is for you because you wanted a kitten." He lowered the bags to the floor, and then he sat crossed-legged next to his daughter. "I did apologize to your mother for the kitten. I should have told her about the kitten and made sure it was okay with her."

"But you did it anyway."

"I did, and that was wrong."

Junie tilted her head to the side and gave him a long, careful look. "So, I should never do what you do."

"Never! You're a much better person than I am."

"I love you, Daddy."

"I love you, too, June Bug. I love you so much." Pieces of his heart seemed to fit back into place, pieces he hadn't realized were missing. This child and her love, she was like a healing balm.

"Will you come see me soon?"

"I will. Every chance I get, I'll be here."

"I'm glad. I don't want to miss you."

He pulled her close. "I don't want to miss you, either."

Together, they assembled the cat tower. They found a place for the litterbox and filled it. Next, they filled the water and food dishes. The kitten, gray and fluffy, followed them, watching with curious blue eyes.

"I named him Smoky." She picked the kitten up and sat him on the carpet-covered tower. "He's a king, and this is his castle."

Fifteen minutes earlier, the king had been dressed

and diapered and riding in a stroller. His daughter had imagination. She was a wonder to him.

"Are you going back to my grandpa's house tonight?" Junie asked as they walked back downstairs.

"I am. Your mom is ready for peace and quiet."

"And you're not peace and quiet," she said with a sage nod of her head.

"I'm definitely neither of those things."

They found Kylie in the sitting room, curled up beneath the blanket he'd draped over her and sound asleep. They stood for a moment, watching the rise and fall of her steady breathing. Mark looked down at his daughter and saw the pucker between her brows, a sign that she had deep thoughts or worries.

"I'll be fine," Junie said out of nowhere. Was she convincing him or herself?

"Are you hungry?" They'd eaten at Buck's, but he could use a snack, so he guessed she might need something.

"I'm a little hungry. You don't have to stay." She said it in her "I'm almost grown" voice.

"I'll stay. Let me get her to bed. Where's her room?"

"Should you?" Junie asked, still the mature adult version of a six-year-old.

"I should."

"I'll show you. First, I'll pull back the blankets."

She hurried down the hall and returned moments later. Mark scooped Kylie up in his arms, relishing the feel of her, the way her head easily nestled against his shoulder and her arms went around his neck. Her breath, soft and warm, brushed against his cheek.

"She's heavy," Junie said.

"Shhh, she isn't. Lead the way."

Junie trotted off, the kitten held loosely in her arm,

bouncing as she skipped her way down the hall, as if this might be the best game ever.

"What are you doing?" Kylie murmured as he put her in bed, pulling the blankets up to her chin.

"Tucking you in," he said. "Do you want me to sing to you?"

"You used to sing for me," she whispered. "Please don't sing."

"I won't."

"You can go. I'll be fine."

He glanced back, searching for their daughter. She'd disappeared. Smart girl, she knew to give them space.

"Junie doesn't want to be alone."

"I'm fine. I can get up."

"You've been up, and now you're exhausted. Go to sleep, Kylie. I've got this."

Her eyes closed, but not before he saw pain and memories reflected in her expression. *Go on. I've got this.* Junie had been a baby, and Kylie had left her with him. He'd said that exact same thing, and he'd let her down. She'd come home to a crying, hungry baby and a husband who didn't know where he was. He couldn't ask her to trust him, not when he'd been that man.

"I was a fool," he whispered now. "I can apologize a million times, but I can't take back the things I've done. More than anything, I want you to be able to trust me. I'm sober. I'm going to stay sober."

They'd traveled to a new place, both of them, but separately. She'd found independence and her own life, a life of stability and peace. He'd found peace in sobriety. Parallel lives, not meeting, but side-by-side, going in their own directions together.

"I want you to stay sober." It took a few minutes for her to get the words out. He'd watched her try to find what it was she wanted to say.

"But it's hard to trust."

She nodded. "I'm trying."

"I know you are. Go to sleep, and please try to trust me with this. I won't hurt her or you."

He bent to kiss her cheek, and then he brushed back the silvery tresses that fell forward, soft like silk. Cherished. She should always and forever feel cherished. Someone better would come along.

"You should go," she said. "We'll be fine."

"I know you will, but I'm here. I'll get Junie settled in for the night."

"And the cat."

He grinned at that. "Forgive me for the cat?"

"It's going to require penance."

If it made her smile, he'd do penance every day of his life. Instead, he'd do the night shift so she could rest knowing that their daughter was taken care of.

Chapter Eight

Singing. Junie's voice and Mark's blended together, his gravelly tones and hers sweet and young. The song had always been one of Kylie's favorites, a song about country roads and wildflowers and love that lasted forever.

She forced herself out of bed, and she gave herself grace because it had been a rough couple of weeks, including the time before the surgery, when she hadn't realized how sick she was. A person couldn't have surgery and, one week later, be back to life as usual.

She needed to get back to the coffee shop. She had to find someone who could work for her while she supervised and perhaps worked the register. She knew she didn't have to worry about money, not really, but Mindy was her mother and her problem, not Mark's. She wouldn't ask him to foot the bill for the assisted living apartment where her mother lived and received daily help from an aide. It was a beautiful place, nicer than anything Mindy had ever lived in.

Drugs had taken their toll, and her mother wasn't mentally healthy. She wasn't physically healthy.

A few minutes later, she followed the singing, now a silly childhood song, to the kitchen. They were cooking together. Junie perched on a stool and Mark next to her, telling her to whip that batter up.

"You're going to make a mess of my kitchen." Kylie immediately regretted the words. Junie looked so happy, standing next to her daddy, the whisk ready to "whip that batter." Now her look changed to crestfallen, and Kylie knew that she'd taken something special from her daughter.

She looked at her normally immaculate kitchen, now cluttered with dishes and spills. She liked neat and tidy. The mess nearly made her skin crawl.

But Junie.

Why didn't she bake with her daughter? She used to, before the coffee shop had gotten so busy. It used to be a thing they did together.

"We're making breakfast." Mark used a calm, "step quietly and it won't bite" voice.

Kylie took a few deep breaths and found a smile, for her daughter and for Mark. "Carry on."

"You mean it?" Junie asked.

"I mean it. Clean up when you're finished and don't forget to touch the center of your pancake, just lightly, to make sure it's cooked all the way through."

"If it pushes in, it's mushy." Junie remembered what Kylie had taught her. It made her feel lighter on the inside, to know she could do this. She could let them make their mess. Her world wouldn't fall apart. Later, if the cleaning job didn't meet her standards, she could tidy up.

A dirty kitchen didn't equal her life falling apart.

"We're going to church together," Junie called out as Kylie poured herself a cup of coffee.

"I know. Do you have clothes picked out?"

Junie nodded, and then she licked batter off her hand.

Kylie cringed, and Mark caught her eye and winked. They used to make breakfast together, the two of them in their tiny apartment. When had they stopped?

When the apartment became a part of their struggling past? She thought that had to be the case. They moved from that apartment to a pretty house in a gated community on the outskirts of Nashville.

She remembered the kitchen in that big house. It had been a modern wonder with all the bells and whistles of a customized home. She'd loved that kitchen, and she'd kept it spotless. They'd stopped cooking together, and then they'd stopped eating together.

They'd stopped going to church together.

"Go sit down with your coffee." Mark said it cheerfully, but she heard the worry in his tone.

"Thank you." She wandered to her sitting room, still lost in thought. For several minutes, she stood at the windows, looking out at her lawn and wishing for spring, for green grass and flowers. A movement caught her attention. She froze, her coffee cup lifted to her lips, and she watched deer, three of them, wander through her yard. They were nervous, ears twitching, occasionally reaching for a bite of grass.

They were beautiful.

"Mommy, the pancakes are finished. We'll bring you a plate," Junie's chipper voice called out. The deer darted away.

"We'll eat together in the dining room."

The room, furnished with a beautiful white table that gleamed beneath the chandelier, rarely got used. She and Junie typically sat at the bar in the kitchen.

They should eat together.

"Can we really?" Junie called out.

The joy in her tone brought a smile to Kylie's face.

Eating together, such a simple thing, and yet it brought so much happiness.

"Yes, of course we can."

She joined them in the kitchen. The pancakes were a little on the brown side. The bacon had been microwaved. The syrup had been poured into a tiny pitcher and heated, drips running down the sides. One of the vases of flowers had been moved to the center of the dining-room table. The flowers were a riot of colors, a mixture of roses and other cut flowers. Daisies, zinnias and lilies.

"This is really nice." She surveyed their hard work, and then she gave her daughter a hug, holding her close for a long moment. "I love you so much."

"I love you, too, Mommy. Do you like our breakfast?"

"I think it might be the best breakfast ever." She hugged her again and let her go.

Junie hurried to a seat. Mark pulled out the chair at the head of the table and motioned for her to sit. "We made orange juice."

"Wow, that's wonderful."

He winked. "I'm sure it's the best."

The wink might have been a warning. It didn't matter. The few seeds in the orange juice didn't matter. The crispy edges of the pancakes didn't matter. What mattered was the three of them sitting down together, Mark bowing his head to pray over their meal, Junie glowing with happiness. Those things mattered.

For that reason, it might have been the best breakfast ever.

"We should do this every Sunday." Junie made the announcement after breakfast, as they cleared the table.

"That isn't possible. We live here. Your daddy lives in Nashville. He has a job there."

Mark picked Junie up and sat her on the countertop. "I will do everything in my power to be here as many Sundays as possible. If your mom approves, we can share Sunday breakfast responsibilities. We can have breakfast at Grandpa Buck's or here. We'll cook together and clean up together."

"And go to church together?" Junie wanted to know. Her nose scrunched as she gave his plan serious consideration.

"Your mom and I will work out the details."

She wished he'd thought about that before he made his plan, but Mark had always been impulsive. Not that his plan didn't have merit; it did. They could have separate lives but co-parent in a way that made Junie feel safe and loved.

How it made her feel, that was another matter altogether.

Junie looked from her father to her mother, and then she hopped down from the counter, a mighty jump for a little girl. Her eyes widened as she landed, and she looked proud of her accomplishment.

"I'm going to get ready for church. You two should hurry."

"We'll hurry," Mark promised. "I have to run to the ranch to change, but I'll be back in time to get you for church."

"Promise?" Junie asked, sticking out her pinky for him to hook his through.

"Promise."

Junie hugged his waist, and then she skipped away, singing her silly song from earlier.

"I shouldn't have done that." Mark sighed. "I get so

caught up in being here, in being in her life, and I forget that we're not…"

"We're a family, Mark. We're not a couple."

"I have to go back to Nashville. I have meetings. I really don't want to leave you without help."

"I'll ask at church. I'm sure someone can help. When will you be back?"

"Probably the first week of February. I promised to help your committee, and I'm not going to leave them high and dry. I have a fantastic idea that I'm going to discuss with them today."

She couldn't help but laugh. "I'd like to see you in a committee meeting with those ladies."

"Hey, I'm a good idea man."

"Oh, no doubt. It's just you and the committee—you're you, they're them. It's amusing."

"A little amusing," he agreed before going all serious. "I hate leaving you. I know you're still recovering."

"I'm fine. I really can take care of myself. I can also take care of Junie."

"I know you can, but you're not allowed to drive for another week."

"I have friends here."

Something she hadn't really had in Nashville. Not real friends. Here, she had people she could count on. People she trusted.

"I'm glad." He took a step closer. "I really want to hug you."

"Hug me?" It seemed a strange request.

He gave a casual shrug. "Yeah, a hug. Just a hug."

She could really use a hug. She took a step closer, giving permission without saying the words. His arms, strong and always comforting, wrapped around her and pulled her close. She could feel his warmth, smell his woodsy scent. She leaned against his shoulder, wishing they could go back and do things right, better. If only they'd gotten help before it was too late.

If they hadn't done things and said things that couldn't be taken back, maybe they would have a chance at fixing their marriage. The things that had happened had ended them. Relationships didn't have a rewind, only a forward. And going forward was all Kylie had in her. She had to live each day in the present, for herself and for Junie. Mark being back in their lives changed everything. She had to learn to let him in without letting him break her heart again.

The parking lot of Sunset Ridge Community Church now had an overflow section. Matthew would say that God had brought the people. Maybe it had something to do with the gift God had given Matthew. He knew how to bring a message that changed lives.

Mark parked and got out to open the passenger door for Kylie. She hurried to remove herself from the truck, giving him a cheeky grin in the process.

"I'm very accomplished at door opening," she informed him.

"Buck didn't teach us much, but he did teach us that a man opens doors for women."

"Is this an argument?" Junie hurried between them, grabbing up Mark's hand and Kylie's and skipping between them. He'd come to realize his daughter didn't have a slow speed. Junie always seemed to be on the move.

He had also realized back at the house that she'd shoved the kitten in her backpack purse. He'd almost let her get away with it, but then realized that might not be a parenting "do." So he'd told her that Smoky might not appreciate church, especially if she escaped and got lost. She'd carried the kitten back upstairs and returned moments later with her backpack empty except for a coloring book and crayons.

"Good catch," Kylie had whispered.

"This is not an argument," Kylie informed their daughter now. "We just have different opinions."

"So I should open my own doors?" Junie asked.

Mark gave Kylie a look, feeling a bit smug as he did.

"You are fully capable of opening your own doors. You may also like to let men or boys open doors for you. It isn't at all bad for a young man to be a gentleman and to show a woman or girl that she is special."

"Thank you, Mommy." Junie slipped free from their hands. "I like to be special, and I like when Daddy opens the doors. Sometimes doors are heavy. I'm going to find Aunt Parker."

"Make sure you don't interrupt her if she's busy," Kylie warned. And then to him. "She's not wrong— doors can be heavy."

Man, she was beautiful. Her eyes were luminous and tilted just a bit at the corners, and she always knew how to wear her makeup without covering up her natural beauty. She was taller than average, and he only had a few inches on her, so she always seemed to be looking right at him when she talked to him. The moment made him want to reach for her hand, but he knew now wasn't the time or place.

"Mark?" She sounded a bit concerned.

"Just thinking."

"About Junie?" she asked.

He chuckled. "Nah, about you and how beautiful you are."

"Stop."

He did, but he caught the quick tilt of her lips. She might say to stop, but she still loved a compliment. They entered the church together, causing multiple heads to turn in their direction. Mark understood how small-town life worked. By evening, everyone would have a different version of their story, speculation would roam free. Were they together? Were they not? Would he stay or go?

A few would question how long he'd stay sober. After all, everyone knew Buck, and the apple didn't fall far from the tree.

He knew he should think better of people, but he was a product of Sunset Ridge, and he knew how the gossip chain went and the things people said. Not that Buck, and even the four brothers, hadn't given people reason to talk.

They sat next to Buck, Parker and, of course, Junie. She had cuddled up between her grandfather and her aunt Parker. Envy sprouted again, like a noxious weed that insisted on coming up. Due to his absence—and he had no one to blame but himself—Junie had a bond with her grandfather that she didn't have with him. Buck had changed, and he'd proven himself to Junie and even to Kylie.

Buck had managed real change. That gave Mark hope.

In the absence of a music minister, the worship service that morning was led by the youth-group choir. The church pianist did her best to keep up with the guitar and drums brought in by the teens, and she smiled as the trio, two teen girls and a teen boy, led the singing. Mark couldn't be sorry that he'd said no to his brother. The teens did a terrific job, and the congregation—although a few looked skeptical or even disapproving at first—rallied and took part.

Matthew came forward after the song service. Mark had listened to his brother's sermons but rarely sat in church as he preached. The sermon, probably not written with Mark in mind, still seemed directed his way. The verses were intended for husbands. Mark read and reread the Scripture. He'd heard the verses, but he'd never really thought about them. Even now, he wondered how he could ever possibly live up to what Matthew said was the love of God for His church.

"Husbands, love your wives, even as Christ also loved the church, and gave Himself for it."

The verses went on: "He that loveth his wife loveth himself."

He closed his eyes, wondering how often he'd put himself first. His wants. His needs. His career. Everything in their marriage had been about her supporting his dreams, and Mark had taken everything she'd offered and then kept taking.

He'd failed her. He'd failed Junie.

He had failed to be the man God called him to be.

There is forgiveness, a still, small voice whispered to his heart. *It's there for the asking.* As the thoughts came at him, the teen choir began to sing a song about surrender and forgiveness. The two came hand in hand, he realized. Surrender his will, his mistakes, his wants. Find forgiveness. At the cross.

He'd asked his wife to forgive him. He'd come here to make things right. He'd never done as the old hymn said and surrendered all. He stood as the choir sang. Closing his eyes, he sang the words of the song, and he surrendered. To whatever God might have for him, whatever direction God might take him in. He even surrendered his relationship with Kylie because God had a plan that would far surpass his own.

The song ended, and he still stood there, in awe of the presence of peace that had settled over him. Whatever happened, he knew that God had a plan.

People drifted away as he stood lost in thought. They probably thought he'd gone crazy, again. Matthew appeared at his side.

"What does it mean? To love your wife as Christ loves the church?" he asked his brother.

Matthew sat down, and Mark sat next to him. They were alone now.

"I'm not perfect," Mark said. "I'm going to fail. I'm going to struggle. I'll sometimes be selfish. How can I love Kylie as well as God loves His people?"

"You always have taken everything to heart and found yourself lacking," Matthew said, his hands folded in his lap as if he were praying for wisdom. He'd need it for this conversation, Mark could assure him of that.

"I let the chickens out."

"You what?" Matthew shook his head, unable to wrap his mind around the statement.

"Mom's chickens. I let them out, and she left."

"Whoa, wait, are you telling me that you've blamed yourself? You were what? Nine years old? She made her own decisions, Mark. She and Buck were a train wreck, probably from the day they said their I do's."

"Maybe Kylie and I are a similar train wreck."

"Or maybe the two of you didn't have a clue how to be a married couple?"

"How, then? How does a husband love his wife in the same way Christ loves the church?"

"Well, first, you're not perfect, and I don't think that verse expects perfection. It expects selflessness. It requires sacrifice and putting someone else's needs ahead of your own. It requires listening because God listens to us when we come to Him. When we're happy, sad, elated over an achievement or just needing to unburden ourselves, He listens. A good husband is an active listener. Sometimes a fixer, but often just a listener. A Godly husband meets needs, takes the burdens that are too heavy, tends to his spouse when she's unwell, dries her tears when she cries. He sacrifices his own wants to make sure she feels loved and cherished."

"I'm pretty selfish because I hear what you're saying, but then I'm thinking, so I get nothing?"

Matthew guffawed at that. The loud burst echoed in the sanctuary.

"Nah, you're not God, so you're not expected to be entirely selfless. Wives can be very supportive. They nurture. They care for and tend to their families. Whether they work in the house or outside the home, they're nurturers. We all have dreams and ambitions, Mark. It's just finding a way to be intentional in our relationships."

"Intentional." He ruminated on the word for a minute. Had they ever been intentional? Maybe in the beginning. Or maybe they'd been obsessed with each other, who knew. He picked up his phone and searched the word because he needed more. *Intentional* meant deliberate, purposeful. He got it. Maybe he got it.

"What are you going to do?" Matthew asked as he looked at the phone and the word definition. They both knew what he meant by that.

"I have no idea. I'm supposed to leave tomorrow. I hur her, and she forgives me, but she'd be right in thinkin that she can't trust me again. Our marriage ended wh she told me she'd spent a lifetime as Mindy Water daughter, lost in her mother's abuse, neglect and add tion. She wasn't going to spend her marriage repeat the cycle, and she wasn't going to allow Junie to grow up repeating the cycle."

"End the cycles, Mark. For her and for yourself. Prove to her that you can be the man she thought she was marrying, the man God called you to be."

"Who is that man?"

Matthew put an arm around him, the way they'd done as boys. "I guess that's for you to figure out."

"Where do I even begin? I love her, Matthew. I got lost for a while and forgot how important loving her is to me. I don't know, maybe I don't trust myself any more than she trusts me. What if I can't stay sober? What if I get lost in addiction and hurt them worse than I already have? Maybe it's better to be here for them when I can."

"Sounds to me like you have some praying to do."

"Thanks a lot."

Matthew stood, and Mark followed.

"Mark, I can't give you answers. I can't direct your paths."

"Of course not. Truthfully, I know that, but it would make my life a lot easier if you would."

"Even if you're no longer married, be the husband, the man, that you're called to be. You have a lot of decisions to make. Start by putting your wife and daughter first. Someday Junie will fall in love. She'll more than likely get married and have children. What type of man do you want in her life?"

"Not one like me, that's for sure."

"Be the dad she deserves." Matthew smacked him on the back, a little harder than was necessary. "Let's go have lunch."

Mark followed his brother out of the church. People were still gathered outside, small groups in conversation, children playing tag. The weather had turned mild, just above fifty degrees. A warm day for January.

A lady with short gray hair and a determined expression headed his way. He thought about pretending he hadn't seen her, but he'd committed himself to this Valentine's project. He didn't want to back out on them.

"Mrs. Pratt." He said it as if he knew and wasn't guessing.

She preened a bit. "Mr. Rivers. I thought I'd check with you about Valentine's Day."

"I'm glad you mentioned it. If this event is large, do you have thoughts about parking? The square will have to be blocked off for the event."

"Oh, now how did that skip our attention? I hope, judging from that smile on your face, that you have an idea."

"I actually do have an idea." He spread his arm out, indicating the church parking lot. "We can use the church, or churches, if necessary. What I'd really like to do is arrange several carriages to drive people from the parking lot to the event. I'd also like to recommend that we have an area for children. A prince and princess ballroom where they can go with their parents, dance, wear crowns and feel special. Also, if we have children in town who would like to attend but don't have a parent to bring them, what if we have assorted costumes and find out if the churches could bring those children as a church activity?"

"Why, Mr. Rivers, I do love that idea. It's just weeks away, do you think we can find the costumes and the carriages in time?"

"Let me talk to Matthew about the carriages, and I'll take care of costumes. If you could talk to the churches about the use of their parking lots for parking and the carriage rides, that would be helpful. I'd even propose a small dining area with free appetizers, nothing to take away from local restaurants. Perhaps cakes, cookies and chocolate-covered strawberries. Don't you believe that Valentine's Day would be more special if it was about showing love to everyone?"

"Now that's a lovely idea. I'll get back to you in the next day or two. Will you be at the coffee shop?"

"No, I won't. Kylie is on the mend and ready to be back in her shop. But I'll be in touch with you."

What he should have said was that he had to leave. He had a career and meetings. He had a flight to catch the next day. The words failed him because at that moment he saw Junie and Kylie heading his way.

He knew one thing. He couldn't leave. Not yet.

Chapter Nine

The convertible pulled up to the barn, where Mark had just been contemplating putting his foot in the stirrup of the rangy quarter horse. The gelding, a buckskin with a scarred-up face and whites in his eyes that showed his complete distrust and disdain, hadn't stood still the entire time Mark had been saddling him up. He hadn't kicked, but he'd made the threat that he would.

He hadn't left on Monday. He hadn't left Tuesday. He'd stayed at the ranch with Buck, praying and trying to figure things out. Now it was Wednesday, and he hadn't bought another plane ticket. He hadn't rescheduled his meetings, he'd just promised that he would be back in town as soon as possible. He'd given Kylie's illness as an excuse.

"You're not really getting on that animal, are you?" The woman exiting the car had long dark hair, dark sunglasses and a posture that spoke of elegance and attitude.

Jael Rivers, the youngest and most privileged of the five Rivers offspring, rarely visited the ranch. She had a comfy life in Tulsa, the spoiled, almost only child of their mother. She'd taken the charitable job of advocating for children in foster care, probably as a way to pay back the brothers who had almost landed there a time or two. Buck had always managed to get his act together long enough to convince the state workers that he could handle parenting and his boys weren't abused.

"I'm thinking about it." He gave her a sideways glance and shook his head as she picked her way across the bumpy ground in her spikey high heels. City gals. "I'm surprised to see you."

Rather than swinging into the saddle, he planted both feet on the ground and waited for her to speak.

"You asked me for a favor. Since you rarely call and I'm sure you weren't going to visit, I decided to hand deliver rather than send it through the mail."

She was correct in her assumption that he wouldn't have visited. He had no relationship with Izzy, their mother. His relationship with Jael had never been a close one, not that he could blame her for that. She was a little sister he barely knew.

"I remember when they unloaded that horse last year. Matthew bought him as a charity case. He felt sorry for him. Twelve years old and a hard life. He hates people."

"Right now, so do I." The words slipped out and he couldn't take them back, nor did he really understand why he'd said them.

"What cat climbed in your litterbox?" she asked, clearly amused by his bad mood.

The saying did pull a smile from him. It reminded him of Junie when he'd dropped his ex-wife and daughter at their house on Sunday, which was the last time he'd seen them. Junie had immediately gone upstairs to her kitten. Now that he thought about it, she'd barely even hugged him goodbye.

Kylie definitely hadn't hugged him goodbye. She'd

smiled, thanked him for his help and then followed Junie inside.

"At least you still have a sense of humor." Jael teased as she approached the fence, pushing the sunglasses to the top of her head so she could watch. She had their mother's eyes, hazel. More green than hazel. She had Izzy's refined looks, like she just walked off a model's runway.

"I do have a sense of humor. I'm named after a disciple, not a woman who put a stake through a man's head."

"I can't even imagine why she named me Jael," his sister said with an exaggerated shudder.

Mark shrugged. "Jael saved God's people."

"I'm not a Jael." She said it with a hint of anger that surprised him.

A better brother, maybe Matthew, would have asked her what was wrong. Even if he asked, he wouldn't know what advice to give a troubled little sister that he didn't know all that well.

"I'm not much of a disciple," he said, hoping to move the conversation forward.

"You're still here. Are you staying?" she asked.

"I'm just hanging out for a few weeks," he answered. "Eventually I'll have to head back. I'm hiring a new agent."

"The old one got sick of your shenanigans?"

"Something like that." What he didn't want to admit, hadn't told anyone, was that unless he could prove his sobriety and his willingness to present a more wholesome image, he was out. His agent had left him, his label wanted his act cleaned up. They wanted proof that he'd show up and perform. He got it. And he would add the public to the list of people he needed to convince. No one wanted to pay all that money for a concert, just to see him stagger around on stage. His band also deserved better. Everyone in his life deserved more from him than they'd been getting.

"How's Kylie and Junie?"

"They're good. Kylie is healing from the appendectomy."

"Which is why you stayed a little longer than you planned."

"Something like that," he answered again. He pulled the cinch a little tighter. The last thing he wanted was for the saddle to come loose and roll, putting him on the hard Oklahoma ground.

She sighed. "Go ahead, ride that old nag."

He didn't tell her that he'd been buttering this horse up for days. He'd been feeding him treats, brushing him, getting him used to the saddle and showing the horse all the kindness he'd never had before coming to this ranch. It had been good for him, handling the angry horse.

He'd been doing a lot that people weren't aware of. Except Buck.

"That horse seems to almost like you." Jael gave the animal a questioning look. "That's strange."

"We have a lot in common."

"Oh, the horse blew his career and his wife left him?" She said it with a typical "little sister" smirk.

"That's harsh," he pointed out, even though she didn't need to be told.

"Sorry, I should be kinder."

"You could be." He moved the horse in a circle and then brought him to a stop, patted his neck and put a foot in the stirrup. The process made the horse shudder, and he reached back to nip at Mark's boot.

"None of that." He pushed the velvety muzzle back,

and the horse snorted. Mark grabbed the saddle horn and swung himself onto the horse's back.

The gelding twisted a bit and hopped, giving not the best attempt at unseating him. From the fence, where she still watched, Jael laughed and mumbled something about extra grain if the horse would take him for a ride.

"Thanks for the support," he tossed back at her as he held the reins and began to talk sweetly to the old nag. Not a nag, just a horse who'd had some rough times and didn't trust.

He rode the horse around the corral, talking to him the entire time, occasionally giving his neck a firm pat. "Doing good, my friend."

"This is boring," Jael said. "So why did you ask me to make this delivery if you're not going to talk to me?"

"I will. I just want to finish what I started."

He loosened the reins and allowed the horse to trot. Buck had joined Jael at the fence. The two spoke quietly, but Mark's father continued to watch, probably wanting a rodeo the same as his youngest child.

"Your cupcakes are cool and ready to frost," Buck said as Mark and the horse made a third trip around the corral, this time at an easy lope.

"Cupcakes?" Jael asked, her nose scrunching. He didn't have time for her. He kept riding, easing into the jolting rhythm of the horse and trying to find a trot that wouldn't rattle his spine.

"He's a baker now." Buck said it with a sly grin that Mark ignored.

"Is he?" Jael cocked her head to the side and then shrugged. "Whatever floats your boat, big brother."

Mark ignored them and rode the horse across the corral, tying him opposite the two hecklers. He unsaddled the animal and carried the tack into the barn. When he returned, his sister had made her way inside the corral, obviously not caring about those fancy shoes of hers. In that moment, she looked at home, as if she'd grown up on this aging old place, rather than the gated property in Tulsa, the house with a pool, a stable and vinyl fencing.

She hadn't grown up dirt poor like her brothers. She didn't know about fried bologna sandwiches, making do with hand-me-downs and feeling embarrassed because Buck didn't always make it home at night.

He knew that Izzy had offered Buck Rivers money to help care for her sons, and Buck had tossed it back in her face and told her he'd take poverty over her money. Mark had resented that decision. He'd gotten past it, though.

"Why this horse?" she asked, her voice softer, her eyes questioning.

He glanced toward the fence where Buck had remained, not crossing and not getting involved in the conversation.

"He kind of reminds me of myself."

She gave a casual shrug and slid the sunglasses back to her nose. Not before he saw the flash of sympathy and understanding.

"Cupcakes and boxes of costumes that had to be delivered today?"

"For this Valentine's Day thing they're planning in town. I wanted to help." He needed to be a part of this community, a part of his family.

"I'll do whatever I can to help out." Jael picked up the brush and started to help groom the horse.

"I'd rather do the grooming. We're building trust. But if you want to join me at the bakery, I'm going to head that way. I have a lot to figure out and a lot to do in the next few weeks."

"Sure, why not since you've already got me here."

"I do appreciate it." He gave her a careful look, the little sister he didn't know all that well.

She looked tired and maybe a little sad. He did something he had rarely done, he put an arm around her and gave her a quick hug. She leaned in for a brief moment and then pulled away, her armor back in place.

"Don't get sappy," she said as she headed for the gate. "I'll meet you at the house.

"Jael," he called out after her. "I do appreciate you being here."

She nodded and kept walking.

He had a lot to accomplish in the coming days. He now realized he also had a sister he needed to spend more time with. First things first, Valentine's Day. He wanted to make it special for his daughter, and for Kylie. It wouldn't make up for the times they'd lost, but it would be a memory his daughter would have, a good memory. A memory with him.

And Kylie, maybe she'd think a little more fondly of him if he could be more the man she deserved. He might doubt himself. He didn't doubt God. So maybe if he and God were working together, he'd be a better person.

The call about Mindy had happened an hour earlier, right as Kylie started to think about cooking dinner for herself and Junie. She needed to go check on her mother. She couldn't drive. She'd had no choice but to call Parker and ask for a ride.

They'd called in an order to Chuck's and were going to pick it up and eat on the road.

"Wait, can you take me to my shop?" Kylie pointed across the square. "Why are there lights on in my shop?"

At Kylie's question, Parker gave a little shrug, as

if she didn't have a clue. Something in her expression said she did know.

Kylie spotted the old red-and-white truck. "What's he doing here?"

"Umm," Parker said.

From the back seat, Faith grew fussy, and Junie said something to her about having a special toy that would make her feel better. A rustle of bags and then a twisting sound. The car filled with the sound of "Wildwood Flower." It was a tinny dulcimer sound and Loretta's voice singing of her lost love.

The song had been based on a poem that she'd memorized as a child. "I'll Twine 'Mid the Ringlets." It was melancholy but beautiful, telling of a love that had gone sadly wrong.

He taught me to love him, he called me his flower...

She started to tell Junie to put the music box away, but Faith giggled and cooed, no longer sad. The song didn't usually bring cheer. Years ago, Mark had found an old dulcimer in the attic of his home, and he'd learned to play just that one song on the instrument. She'd learned to sing, just to accompany him.

Years later, he'd taken her to the Opry, and Loretta had been there. She'd signed the old dulcimer for them. She didn't know where the instrument had gone to, but she'd cherished it until it had seemed like a part of their demise.

My visions of love had all flown away...

She needed a new song. A song that brought memories that cheered her, not took her down a dark path of the past.

"I don't have time for this, but I need to talk to him."

"I thought you might." Parker pulled into a space and killed the engine of her car. "Want me to wait?"

"I don't know. Yes. Maybe. Why is he here? Is that man ever going to leave?"

"My guess is he doesn't even know why he's still here." Parker nodded toward the coffee shop. "Go. Junie and I will run over and get our orders from Chuck's."

"That works for me." Kylie sighed, too tired to deal with whatever Mark might be up to.

Since the surgery, she'd felt as if she couldn't overcome the constant exhaustion. She just wanted to be better and to get back to her life. Her very uncomplicated, un-Mark life.

"Here's a twenty for our dinner." She pulled the money from her pocket and got out of the car.

Her shop was unlocked. She pushed the door open and went inside. From the kitchen, she could hear him singing a Kenny Chesney song. He'd always loved Kenny. Someone else spoke, a woman.

"Hello," Kylie called out as she entered the kitchen.

Mark dropped a tube filled with pink icing, and the pink went everywhere. The woman standing next to him, a brunette with pretty green eyes, had the grace to flush a deep red.

"Oh, you weren't supposed to be here." Mark swiped his finger through the icing and tasted it.

"Was I not? As far as I know, it's still my coffee shop. If memory serves, you're the one who shouldn't be here. I thought you were flying out. You had meetings."

"And you didn't have anyone to help you so I stayed. I've been at the ranch, working on perfecting these cupcakes." He said it gently, as if she might be on the verge of a breakdown. She wasn't. She was absolutely in control of her emotions. "I wanted to help."

"And it appears you found help." She gave the woman a pointed look.

"Oh, you don't recognize me." The woman spoke, flashing white teeth and dimples. Those Rivers dimples. She didn't have the silvery gray eyes.

"Jael." Kylie felt like a fool. "You've done something with your hair."

"I let it go back to its natural color, and I stopped perming."

"Oh, I see." She'd been upset to think he had a woman here. She shouldn't have let it bother her. They'd been over for years. Divorced for three.

"I wanted to surprise you." Mark moved, giving her a clear view of the cupcakes. She stepped closer, inspecting the cakes with their swirled pink icing. "Ta-da!"

"Goodness." She wouldn't classify herself as speechless, but nearly speechless might describe it.

"They taste as good as they look." Jael picked one up and handed it to her. "Buck and Mark make a pretty decent baking team."

"I never thought about having cupcakes, I mean, other than the ones you burned last week."

"Cupcakes are always well received," Jael said with a wink. "Go ahead, take a bite. I had one, and I feel fine."

Kylie licked the icing, ignoring the wide-eyed look on Mark's face. Ignoring, but enjoying. She took a little bite, closing her eyes at the sweetness and the flavor. "This is amazing. The flavor is very unique."

"You'd be surprised." Mark gave a little chuckle as he picked up the tube and began to ice the rest of the cupcakes.

"What is it?"

His brow arched, and he flashed those dimples.

"Strawberry and lime with strawberry icing."

"I never would have thought to put those flavors together."

"It's what Buck had in the kitchen, so I used it. It turned out really good."

"It's very good."

She looked at her watch. "I have to go."

"Where are you going?" he asked as he frosted another cupcake.

"My mom is a mess, and they're transporting her to the hospital for an evaluation. I'm not sure what they're going to do with her."

"Let me take you." He carried the icing tube to the sink and ran hot water through it. "I can have this cleaned up in a jiffy."

"You didn't make a mess of my kitchen."

"I baked these at Buck's. His kitchen didn't fare so well. I might be able to bake—a talent I didn't realize I had—but I'm not doing a great job of being a neat chef."

"Parker would probably appreciate it if you could take me. Faith is teething and fussy. But do we have to take that old truck? The exhaust fumes…"

"Take my car," Jael offered as she pulled keys out of her pocket. "I'll drive the truck back to the ranch. I can also take Junie with me. We haven't spent a lot of time together, but I know we could have fun."

The offer took Kylie by surprise, and it also caused a little apprehension. She didn't know Jael, not really. Junie didn't know her that well. What she did know about Jael was that she worked for the state as an advocate for children in state's custody. She was young for a job that carried so much responsibility. Parker had told her that Jael had gone back to school and was getting a degree in psychology in order to better help the children.

"Let's see how Junie feels about that," Mark suggested, and she nodded, hoping he understood how much she appreciated his insight.

When Parker returned, they asked Junie, and she loved the idea of going with her very fun and very cool aunt. As she got out of the car, she leaned in to kiss Faith, and then she pulled the music box out of the bag and started telling her aunt Jael the story of how her daddy bought her this music box and how her mommy had actually met Loretta at the Grand Ole Opry.

"You're sure you don't want me to take you?" Parker asked, even as Faith began to whimper.

"Go home and take care of your daughter. I'll be fine." She would be fine.

It made sense that Mark would take her. He knew her mother, knew the childhood and teen years that Kylie had survived with her parent. It made sense, and yet it created a thread between them, binding them. They had their past, not just their marriage, but a childhood of being friends, of him being there for her, caring for her. All of that past had a way of getting tangled up. The childhood trauma, the love they'd shared, the pain he'd caused.

Yet there he stood, that best friend again, making sure she had someone on her side.

He was on her side.

"Stop frowning." He had backed Jael's car out of the parking space, and now he was reaching for Kylie's hand.

"Why can't life be simple?"

"Because it's life. Because it's messy and unpredictable and full of surprises."

"Like you not leaving town," she said, half accusing and half thankful that he hadn't left. For Junie's sake, she told herself. Junie had been distraught over his departure.

"Where are we heading?" Mark asked as they drove out of town.

"I'll put the address in the GPS." She leaned in and gave the screen on the dash a careful look. "If I can figure it out."

She fiddled with the navigation system and finally got the address entered. "Thirty minutes. They haven't transported her to the hospital just yet. I want to make sure the right decision is being made."

"I know this is tough, but you're tougher than any situation you've encountered. You survived her, and you survived me. Honestly, no one should have to be this strong, Kylie. You deserve better."

Tears stung her eyes, but she wouldn't let them fall. She would not cry at the sweetness of his words, the way he said them making her wish they could have been better together. Would a stronger person have stayed with him, seeing him through the hard times?

Would a stronger person have put her mom in a home or brought Mindy to live in her house? A strong person held on to the people they loved and carried them when they were at their weakest.

"Stop!" Mark gave her hand a squeeze.

"Stop what?"

"Overthinking," he said, still holding her hand. "Don't doubt that you're one of the most loving, amazing people on this planet."

"How can you say that?"

"Because I've known your love, and I miss it every single day."

She blinked, but she couldn't stop the tears that trickled down her cheeks. She brushed them away, but more took their place. He always knew the right words, the words that went straight to her heart.

"I can't have this conversation right now," she told him. "I'm too emotional, too tired."

"Take a nap. The GPS will get us where we need to go. And Kylie, I want you to know, I'm praying that I can be a better man, for you and for Junie. I'm still here because I need to find a way to do that for you."

She shook her head, trying to cut off his words. "No. That isn't the direction we're going. I can't go back, not to that life, not to Nashville and not to the fear of losing you again."

"I know that." He said it so calmly. "I'm going to be the best version of myself for the two of you because that's what I'm called to do. This has nothing to do with going back. It doesn't have anything to do with uprooting you from your life."

Words, she reminded herself. He'd always been so good with words. Actions were what mattered.

Actions mattered, and she couldn't deny that he'd been there for her. In the past two weeks, he'd taken care of her, taken care of Junie. The man had even taught himself to bake and to make lattes. She couldn't help but smile as she dozed off.

Thirty minutes later, she roused herself from a short nap as the GPS announced their destination. They were pulling into the parking space in front of the apartment her mother had called home for the past two years. From inside came shouting and then laughter.

Kylie froze on the front step. She didn't want to go inside, to face her mother in this condition. Mark reached past her and opened the door. He stepped inside, holding her hand, tethering her to him and to his strength.

"What are you doing here?" Mindy Waters spoke with harsh tones, her expression wild as she faced her daughter. "I thought you dropped off the face of the earth again. Always a disappointment."

"I've been sick." She held tight to Mark, but she took deep breaths, calming herself. She reminded herself that her mother couldn't help it. Mindy had never been mentally healthy. She had a disease. As clearly as a physical illness, Mindy's illness mattered.

"Mom, they can't allow you to stay in this apartment if you're going to sneak out and use."

"I'm not using. They're lying to you. They say that stuff because they know that I know what they're doing here. They're stealing my money."

"Mom..." Kylie sighed her frustration.

"You could take me to your house. To his big fancy house." By "his," they both knew that Mindy meant the man who was her father.

Kylie couldn't take her mother to that house. She wasn't a bad daughter or unfeeling, but she knew how Mindy's presence would change things, how it would affect Junie. She wouldn't subject her daughter to this behavior.

Every decision she made, no matter how difficult, had to be about her daughter. Their daughter. She leaned a little in Mark's direction, finding strength in his presence.

"Mom, I think you have to go to the hospital. You're going to need to be evaluated."

"I'm not going."

"You are, Ms. Waters. We've called an ambulance and the police." The nurse moved toward the door, as if she knew Mindy's next move. Fortunately, Mark also moved in that direction. "Ms. Waters, you can't leave."

Mindy began to pick things up and throw them, smashing her knickknacks on the floor. Her puppy dog collection, her Christmas ornaments that she insisted on keeping out year-round and an ashtray she'd had forever because it had been her mother's. She screamed, demanding to be set free.

Kylie felt the exhaustion again, so heavy and so hard to fight. This battle with her mother had been lifelong. It had humiliated her, enraged her, made her run away as soon as she graduated high school.

Now it made her want to weep with compassion because Mindy Waters would never be healthy. She would never know true happiness or contentment.

But God...

She closed her eyes for a few seconds, letting that thought wash over her and give her peace.

She needed that peace as the police came and then the ambulance. Mindy didn't go willingly. She ranted and raved that her daughter should stop them from taking her. Then she started a new tactic, blaming Kylie, yelling that this had been Kylie's plan all along.

They closed the ambulance doors. The police spoke to Kylie for a few minutes, and then they left. The nurse apologized for how difficult the situation had been, and she too left.

Mark remained.

He encircled her in his arms, the way he'd done on so many similar occasions in her life. He held her as she sobbed, finally letting go and letting the tears come. His hand on her back felt firm and strong. He had been and could still be her anchor.

She needed his strength. Today.

"Let's take the back roads home," he suggested after a few minutes of her just leaning against him, breathing.

"Why?"

"Because it's what we used to do when we needed

time away from them. We'll take the back roads and open the windows to let the breeze blow in. I'll buy you a burger at Chuck's, and we'll share an order of fries and a milkshake."

"I don't want to share," she whispered against his shoulder. "You're not that poor Rivers boy anymore. I want my own fries and my own strawberry shake."

"I thought you liked chocolate."

She sniffled and then giggled. "No, you like chocolate. I never told you that I prefer strawberry."

He pressed his lips against the side of her head, his cheek then resting there. "Silly girl. You should have told me."

There were a lot of things she'd never told him. She'd never told him that she had always feared she would become like her mother. Her need for a clean, tidy house with no pets went far beyond simply being a clean person. She feared chaos and messiness because what if she let go of her strict and orderly life and everything crumbled and she became Mindy?

On the car ride home, he did indeed take the back roads. And even though it was cold, he rolled the windows down to let the cool breeze blow through the car. For a long time, he remained silent, giving her space and a chance to process everything that had happened.

After a while, she told him her fears and why she needed her home to be in order, why his messes and chaos disturbed her. She explained about the cat because what if one cat became two, then three or four?

He pulled off the paved road onto a dirt road and told her she would never be Mindy. She was strong and good, and even if her life got messy and a cat roamed her house, she would still be Kylie.

He stopped the car, pulling to the grassy shoulder.

"I can't do this," she told him as tears trickled down her cheeks. "I can't be strong for everyone."

"Let me be strong for you. Let me hold you."

She nodded and he pulled her close, holding her as his hands caressed her back. She looked up to tell him how glad she was that he'd driven her.

He kissed her then, and she kissed him back, and she wished they could have been different together.

Chapter Ten

Mark picked Kylie up Thursday morning. They were going to the coffee shop together. Junie climbed in the seat between them, still groggy and complaining that the sun hadn't come up. He ruffled her hair and told her she could sleep on the cot in the back room of the coffee shop. It was a new addition, something he'd bought for her. After all, little girls needed their sleep.

The drive took only a few minutes, but Junie dozed against him. Kylie sat quietly, watching out the window, not looking at him. Because yesterday he'd parked on a back road and kissed her. Not one of his best moments, not when he had made a decision to prove himself to be a trustworthy friend. She hadn't called him out, not really, but she'd grown distant on the drive back to the ranch, where she'd collected Junie and asked for a ride home.

He parked down the block from the coffee shop, saving spaces out front for the customers.

"It's dark," Junie grumbled as they got out and started in the direction of the coffee shop. "And cold."

"It is cold," Kylie agreed, and she pulled their daughter a little closer to her side. "It'll be warm inside the shop."

"I hope so," Junie said, teeth chattering.

Kylie unlocked the door, and they rushed inside, where it was indeed warmer than outside, but not the kind of warm they needed. Mark headed for the thermostat, while Kylie started the morning routine of preparing the coffeemaker before she began the baking process.

"It's good to be back," Kylie said as she started the coffee. "I've missed my customers and my days here."

"I'm sure they've missed your cooking." Mark entered her space behind the counter and saw her physically tense up. He'd done that. The kiss had been impulsive and careless, he realized. She'd been vulnerable and in need of comfort. He should have given his actions more thought.

After checking on Junie, he came back and shared those thoughts with her. "I should have been a better friend to you yesterday."

"What does that mean?"

"I thought the back roads, some fresh air, that it would help you to relax. And then I let the memories swoop in. Kissing you has always been second nature, it seems."

"Mark, I let you kiss me. You're not guilty here, unless we're both guilty. I feel like I need to apologize because I don't want to mislead you."

"I'm not misled. We should both let it go and stop worrying."

She seemed to agree with him. The expression on her face brightened, and her eyes reflected humor rather than the troubled look she'd worn since yesterday.

"Thank you, for being with me yesterday. And for the drive down memory lane."

"Anytime," he assured her. "I'm your huckleberry."

"I'm not even sure what that means."

The moment lightened their moods and eased the tension between them. They'd always been good together, until they hadn't. They'd shared their silly jokes and found ways to get through the difficult times.

Until they hadn't.

"Same. We'll have to do some research. What if it means something like I'm going to eat your cookie or take the last piece of cake?"

She already had her phone out, and she shook her head, disagreeing with his nonsense ideas. "It might have come from King Arthur's court, something about how a huckleberry scarf on a sword meant the knight swore allegiance." Her voice had trailed off as she read. Slowly, her gaze lifted to meet him.

"I'm your huckleberry," he repeated.

She shook her head and walked away. He had a bad habit of going too far, he realized, and it hinted at desperation.

"Stop trying so hard," she told him from the kitchen, where she'd pulled out a couple of cartons of eggs. "I'm going to make quiche. You should watch and learn."

"That's probably a good idea. Someday I might want to make you breakfast."

"Stop." She cracked an egg and emptied it into a bowl. The next egg followed. And the next.

"Can I help?"

She slid the bowl between them and then passed him a dozen eggs.

"Try not to get shells in the bowl." She watched as he cracked an egg and opened it above the bowl. No shells. He couldn't help but feel a little proud of the accomplishment. He didn't want to tell her that there might be tiny pieces of eggshell in the cupcakes.

"I don't know what to do about my mom." She'd been

silent as she added eggs to the bowl. Now she leaned against the counter and watched as he finished up. "I should go see her. Why does the idea of visiting cause me to be so anxious? And then anxiety turns to guilt."

"Trauma does that to us." He finished his eggs and wiped his hands on a wet towel she'd placed on the counter. "The brain of a child who has suffered trauma is not the same as the brain of a child who had a fairly functional and happy childhood. I'm guessing the idea of seeing Mindy sends your brain into fight-or-flight mode. Growing up, you never knew what Mindy you were waking up to, or what you'd find when you came home from school. Or who you'd find. That kept you stressed out and in a constant state of coping with your life."

"You didn't have it much better."

"I had my brothers, and I always knew I'd have a home."

She slipped her hand into his. "And I always knew that I had you."

He gave her hand a light squeeze. "I let you down. I'm going to do everything in my power to make sure that never happens again."

She didn't respond, and he shouldn't have expected anything from her. Maybe she had the same response to him that she had to her mother.

"If you want me to go with you to see her, I will."

"Maybe," she said. She had slipped her hand free from his and now stood at the fridge with the door open. "What did I want from here?"

"One of my amazing cupcakes?"

She shook her head. "Not this early in the morning. Oh, ingredients for the quiche."

He glanced at the clock on the wall. "Should I turn on the lights and open up?"

"That would be good. If we have customers, the quiche will be ready in thirty minutes. I have French toast, too."

She'd mixed the ingredients at her house before they'd left. Eggs, cream, vanilla, a little sugar and a dash of salt. He had always loved watching her cook and eating her creations. It made sense that she would have this place with her name on it.

The first customers were already at the door, waiting to be let in. He ushered them inside to the warmth of the coffee shop. Kylie came out of the kitchen, drying her hands on a towel. Her welcoming look for the customers almost brought him to his knees. The way her face lit up when she saw her people, her customers, it made him a little envious.

He wanted that look for himself.

"Diana and Cora, it's so good to see you all." She moved around the counter to give the two ladies a quick embrace. "What can I get for you today?"

"We're so glad to see you open again. We were on our way to work and thought we'd make a turn around the square, just in case." This from the lady with a very immaculate shoulder-length hairdo.

He guessed from Kylie's greeting that she was Diana and the other woman was Cora.

The woman, Diana, gave him a sharp look. That brought a moment of discomfort. He could hurry to the back, pretending to help cook, or he could smile and move past what was probably well-deserved censure. Truth be told, he'd been deserving of more than those caustic looks.

Kylie grabbed an order pad.

Watching her, he saw what others probably did not. She put on a good front, but she still needed time to recover. Time that she wouldn't take because she knew that he would be leaving and because this coffee shop meant freedom from him.

After taking the order, she hurried to the kitchen and proceeded to make the French toast and bacon that her customers had ordered.

"Let me help." He moved in close. "If I can grill a PB and J, I can make French toast. Tell me what to do."

He thought she'd tell him that she could do it herself. Instead, she stepped aside and motioned toward the loaf of bread and the dish containing the dipping ingredients.

"Soak the bread, but not too long or it will fall apart. The key is just enough."

"What is just enough?" he asked, amused because no one could describe "just enough." He'd grown up with Buck telling him, "Do it until it's finished. You'll be able to tell."

Maybe Buck, who'd become quite a cook, should be the one helping.

"You'll know."

He chuckled at the answer.

"What's so funny?"

"I just knew that's what you'd say. Okay, I'll know. And then?"

"Put it on the griddle, not too hot. It needs to cook all the way through, not just get toasty on the outside."

"I can do this. You make the coffee, and I'll play chef. I wish I had a chef's hat."

"Is that a dream of yours?" she asked as she turned to go. She stopped and opened an overhead cabinet. For a moment, she rummaged and he ignored her because French toast seemed to be finicky and he didn't want to mess up.

She touched his head, and he realized she was putting a hairnet over his hair. And then she giggled and slid a hat on top. He moved his head sideways and felt the sway.

"Is it a real chef's hat?"

"It is. A friend bought it for me, but it seemed a little out of place in Sunset Ridge. But on you, perfection."

"Now I'm legit," he said as he went back to the French toast. "The hat is going to make everything I cook taste better."

"Of course it is." She kissed his cheek and hurried off to make coffee.

He made perfect French toast. He couldn't help but be a little proud of himself. And then a customer came in and ordered his special grilled PB and J. He heard the order and then heard Kylie groan. As someone else ordered the same, he heard her say, "You've got to be kidding me."

"Put it on the menu, Kylie." The customer sounded amused as he made the suggestion.

"You're killing me." She didn't look mad, but she managed a frown as she put in the order. "For real, I'm a classy coffee shop with a small but tasty menu. That's what the *Wagoner* newspaper reported when they did an article on local eating establishments. I have amazing coffee and tasty fare."

"Now you have something no one else has." He winked as he said it.

From the doorway of the inner office, he heard Junie say that she liked his sandwiches a lot. Earlier, he'd put her to work on math and reading, subjects that she breezed through with very little help. She was smart, like her mom. He guessed homeschooling wasn't for everyone, but for his daughter, it seemed to be the right choice.

"I'll make you one," he called out to his daughter.

"It's a mutiny," Kylie laughed as she walked away.

"But you like it," he retaliated.

She stopped at the door to give him a look, one that he couldn't decipher. Maybe because she couldn't decide what she felt about him?

He hoped, no, he prayed, that somewhere in her heart, she was beginning to trust again. If nothing developed between them, if they remained just friends, he wanted to know that her heart had healed and that he could prove himself trustworthy.

They closed at two. Kylie turned off the lights and worked on the dining area, with Junie's help. Mark insisted on doing the dishes and cleaning the kitchen. He wanted to prove himself. She knew that he needed to do this, for himself and probably for her, because he wanted to make her life a little easier.

Her phone rang, and she sat down to answer it. She truly needed to get off her feet. The caller ID showed the name of the hospital. She closed her eyes, waiting for whatever bad news would come. Mindy and bad news were synonymous.

"This is Kylie Rivers," she answered.

"Mrs. Rivers," the person on the other end said. *Mrs.* The title hadn't been hers for several years. "My name is Bailey Jones. I'm calling in regard to your mother, Mindy Waters."

"Yes."

"We have her in our psychiatric unit, and she's sedated but very agitated. She's asking to see you."

"Oh, I see." She must be the worst daughter in the world, but the announcement turned her inside out, making her feel anxious all over again. It had been such a good day, and now this.

A good daughter would tell them she'd be there soon to see her mother. After all, mothers and daughters had bonds. She and Junie had a bond. She prayed they would always be close. She prayed she would never be her mother.

She wasn't her mother. She'd never been Mindy or anything like Mindy.

"Mrs. Rivers?" The woman on the other end questioned, her voice hesitant. "I know this isn't easy. It's never easy to deal with a sick parent."

"No, it isn't easy." She cleared her throat. She tried to find her better self. "Could you tell her that I'll be there tomorrow?"

A hand touched her shoulder, strong and comforting. He massaged the muscles at the back of her neck, and she let her head fall forward. He had a way of releasing the stress. She breathed in, relaxing in his presence.

"I will tell her," Bailey Jones said with a sweet voice of understanding. "Thank you."

"Yes, thank you."

She set her phone down on the counter.

"Let's go to Chuck's for an early dinner," Mark suggested.

"I like that idea. "Thank you, for today and for being here."

"You're welcome. And I'm assuming that call was about visiting Mindy?"

She nodded, resting her head on her arm as she leaned over the table. Exhaustion swamped her, dragging her down, making her entire body feel so heavy. The doctor had warned her that recovery after such a vicious infection would take time. She didn't want it to take time.

"Chuck's special tonight is chicken-fried steak and

mashed potatoes." He tempted in a soft voice, "And I bet he has cherry pie."

"You know how to say all the things a woman wants to hear."

"I'm a romantic." He took hold of her hand, and she should have told him no. She needed to say that they shouldn't because Junie would get the wrong idea. What little girl didn't want her daddy to be the hero? What little girl didn't want a whole family?

Kylie had wanted those things, but her father had been a man who wouldn't claim her. He'd given her mother money that she used for drugs and for her friends who crowded into their tiny trailer.

A trailer that Kylie had spent her childhood trying to clean, always trying to make everything neat and tidy. As if an orderly home meant an orderly life. She'd learned better, and yet she kept trying—was still trying.

She pulled her hand free. "An early dinner sounds good."

"You need to stop feeling guilty." His words jerked her gaze up to meet his, his eyes so light gray, filled with compassion. "She isn't this way because of something you did or didn't do. She's just unwell."

"I know. I really do."

The tap of footsteps, Junie in her boots, meant the conversation needed to end. They parted just as their daughter hurried around the corner of the counter. "Guess what, I checked my spelling, and I got an A."

"Way to go!" Mark swooped her up in his arms. "To celebrate, we're going to Chuck's for dinner. That spelling test deserves a piece of cherry pie."

Kylie couldn't help but make a face. "I'm starting to think you're the one wanting cherry pie, and we're just your excuse. Since it's too early for dinner, maybe we could get pie and ice cream?"

He pulled her close. "You could be right about the pie, but I'm willing to share. Dessert before dinner sounds like a great idea."

"I want a sundae," Junie informed him as she yanked the hat off his head and put it on her own. "Why are you still wearing this silly chef hat?"

"I forgot that I had it on." He pulled off the hairnet that he'd worn under it. "You would have let me go to Chuck's with that on my head."

Kylie smirked at the accusation. "I absolutely would have let you."

Kylie pulled the white hat off her daughter's head and tossed it on a back counter. She grabbed her purse, checked the thermostat and then joined Mark and Junie as they headed out the front door. As she locked the door, she gave the front window a hard look.

"I need more decorations for the Valentine's event. And what is it you're up to for that night? Because I know you're up to something."

He pretended to lock his lips. "Not going to tell, but it's going to be fantastic."

"You'll be here?" She sounded too hopeful and wished she could take back the question.

"I'll be here."

"Can we walk to Chuck's?" Junie asked, wiggling free from her father's arms. He settled her on her feet and she moved between them to take hold of their hands.

She grinned and started to hop forward to swing between their arms, the way she'd done as a toddler.

"No swinging," Kylie warned. "I'm too tired."

Junie sighed her disappointment, but she walked. Or half walked and half skipped.

Chuck's didn't have a big "early dinner" crowd. There were several tables with customers. Of course, in a town like Sunset Ridge, everyone knew everyone else, greeting them as they entered the café with its downhome appeal. Chuck's wife, Jenni Stringer, came out of the kitchen as they entered. She called out to them, telling them to sit wherever they wanted.

Buck, Jael, Matthew and Parker, along with baby Faith, were seated at a large table near the back of the café. Mark led them to the table with his family. The last thing Kylie wanted was for people to assume they were together, but she couldn't shift gears now and ask him to take her home. Junie had already claimed the seat next to Faith. The little girl, now a toddler, banged her cup on the tray of the highchair and reached for Junie. Family. God had indeed made a family for Parker, Matthew and the baby girl that had been abandoned in his truck. They were Junie's family, too. And Kylie knew they considered her a Rivers, still.

She was surprised to see Jael. The younger woman sat next to Buck. She smiled and gave a cheerful greeting to Junie.

Mark pulled out a chair for her, and she accepted, sitting next to Parker. "How are you feeling?" Parker asked.

"Exhausted," Kylie admitted. "I'm obviously better, but the first full day back at work just about knocked me down."

"Take it easy," Parker warned. "You have Mark there to help, so take a seat and order him around."

"And let him cook?" she teased, knowing he would hear, even as he moved to the seat next to his brother.

"I can cook."

"You are improving," she admitted. "And we sold out of the cupcakes he baked."

"Which is why we needed dessert at Chuck's," Mark said. "Now that I'm here, I'm starting to think I'd like more than dessert."

"Mark, did that Realtor get hold of you today?" Buck asked. "She called the house looking for you."

Mark gave a quick shake of his head and cut Buck off. Buck started to speak again, but Mark gave him another pointed look. If he'd just answered, she might not have been so curious. After all, she knew that he planned to find a home in Sunset Ridge, a place of his own for when he came back to visit his daughter.

Matthew asked her a question about the Valentine's Day event and if they had lined up the music and the special menus for each of the local restaurants. Jenni and Chuck's son, Brody, joined him. He didn't ask, but took a seat next to Matthew. Brody had Down syndrome and remained at home with his parents. Everyone in town knew Brody, and Brody knew everyone in town.

"My dad is making heart-shaped cakes for Valentine's Day." Brody played peek-a-boo with Faith as he made the announcement. She giggled, and he chuckled, the sound growly and endearing. "I told him to make steaks and pasta, but he said he wanted steak and shrimp. I don't like shrimp unless it's fried. Do you like shrimp Junie?"

She shook her head. "And I don't like steak."

"What do you like?" Brody asked. "Oh, my mom said to take your order."

"I like chicken strips and fries," Junie answered. "That's what I want today. And chocolate milk. Oh, and a sundae."

"I'll tell my mom," Brody assured her. He scooted back his chair and got up. "Miss Kylie, what can I get you?"

"Are we eating now?" she asked Mark. He shrugged and reached for the menu.

"I guess we are. Those salads at lunch didn't stick with me."

"I'll have the chicken-fried steak, Brody."

"Okay, Miss Kylie." Brody closed his eyes and repeated their orders. Mark started to speak, but Brody gave him a look and walked off.

"Ouch." Matthew sounded amused rather than sorry for his brother. "I think Brody might be mad at you."

"He'll have to get in line, won't he?" Mark answered.

Brody came back a moment later, his features set in contrition. He sighed big when he stopped in front of Mark.

"Mr. Mark, I am sorry for being rude. My mom said I had to say that. She told me to take your order."

"It's okay, Brody. I understand. And I'll have the chicken-fried steak, too."

"Okay. Do you want gravy?"

"I do."

"Chiken-fried steak and gravy." Brody gave him another narrow-eyed look, and then he walked away.

"Sorry, but not." Matthew still sounded amused. "You used to be his favorite."

"His real loyalty is to Kylie, and I don't blame him." Matthew grinned at her, and she flushed.

"What all are you planning for this big Valentine's event?" Buck asked.

Kylie answered. "It will have vendors, lots of twinkling lights, special menus at our restaurants and live music."

"I heard something 'bout…" Buck gave Mark a quick look, winked and closed his mouth on whatever he'd planned to say. "'Bout good cupcakes."

She laughed at the obvious cover up. "Oh, definitely we will have the best cupcakes."

Chuck joined them. He wasn't all that tall, but he was broad shouldered and still wore his hair buzzed as he had in the military. He liked to joke that there was less hair and less color, but he could still pull off the look. Each time he made the statement, Jenni would put an arm around him and kiss his cheek.

She didn't want to envy them, but Kylie could admit that watching Jenni and Chuck grow older and more in love was inspiring. Everyone should want a marriage with that much love and laughter.

Her gaze drifted to the man who sat across the table and down just a few chairs. Mark. He glanced her way, and they shared a look. In moments such as this one, she wanted her marriage back. Her heart wanted to give in and let him back into her life.

Her brain knew better. She knew how this story went. She'd traveled the road with her mother. She'd heard the apologies, lived through brief attempts at making things better, gotten her hopes up. Gotten her heart broken.

Mark had been the one constant in her life. The dependable constant. That was why his decisions had hurt more. She'd relied on him. She'd believed in them as a couple. He'd shown her that the love they shared didn't matter. He'd spent more and more time drinking and less and less time with his family. And then he'd cheated on her with someone she considered a friend.

She could forgive a lot, had forgiven, but now she wasn't sure if she'd forgiven him for that transgression.

Chapter Eleven

Friday afternoon, they left the hospital where Kylie had visited with her mother. Junie had stayed in Sunset Ridge with a friend. Mark had remained in the waiting room. The last thing he'd wanted was to rile Mindy up even more than she already seemed to be.

As they walked across the parking lot to his truck, he could feel the tension between them. Kylie had been reserved, pulling away from him. He knew better than to reach for her. If she needed space, he could give it.

For the moment, it couldn't be about what he wanted or about them. This time was for Kylie to process the situation with her mother.

"How was she?" he asked as he opened the truck door for her.

"Not well." She brushed a hand over her face. "I'm sorry, that answer isn't even close to correct. She's lost. Her memories are fading. She's angry. She's only fifty-eight. She should be living a nice life in a small house, baking cookies with her granddaughter, meeting friends for lunch. Instead, she's being transferred to a facility where they can care for her as her health declines. I hate this for her. I hate it for myself and for Junie."

"It isn't fair," he agreed. "I want to help—I just don't know what to do to make this easier for you."

She climbed in the truck, reaching to close the door. "There's nothing you can do. My mother is a ward of the state. It's a legal decision that I pushed for and got. It is what it is, and we'll get through this."

He climbed in the driver's side and started the truck. As he started to back out of the parking space, she reached for his hand to stop him.

"Today was difficult. It would have been more so without you here. Thank you."

"You're welcome. I just wish I could make it easier."

She shrugged her slim shoulders. "You don't have to. I'm trying to live with a faith like Paul. He said he'd learned to be content no matter his situation. It's crazy to think it, but I am content with my life. I've hit a rough patch, but I'm moving forward with Christ, who strengthens me."

He backed out of the parking space and put them on the road to home. After driving a few minutes, he said, "You're my hero."

He glanced her way, and the sweetness of the expression on her face nearly undid his resolve to remain platonic. She'd had a rough day, but she did manage to look at peace. She looked like everything he'd ever wanted in his life.

"Mark, I have to say something, and it isn't going to be easy."

With those words, she jerked him back to their present situation.

"Okay, whatever you need to say, I'm listening."

"Hmmm," she said. Her expression serene, she spoke. "I forgive you for what you did to me. Not the drinking, the anger, but for cheating on me. I thought I'd forgiven you, but I realized I'd held on to that one. I wanted a reason to stay angry, but staying angry made me bitter, it kept me from having joy. I was only hurting myself."

"I'm sorry." The words were wrenched from him as he tumbled over all the old emotions, the guilt. "I'm not going to blame drinking or say I was in a bad place. I take full responsibility for my actions. They were reprehensible and unforgivable."

"There is no such thing as unforgiveable." She blew out a breath and looked away from him. "That doesn't make it easy to let go of the pain. I've let this be a weight that I've carried for years. I need to surrender my anger and my unforgiveness so I can move on. I'm sorry, but I have to do this for me, not for you."

"I know." He admired her so much. He loved her. He looked up to her for her strength and her faith. She had always been too good for him.

"We have to move forward," she told him as they drove down the back road to Sunset Ridge. No stopping on side roads this time.

"Yes, we do."

"Not together, but as friends."

"I agree." He didn't, not completely, but if he didn't agree, she'd pull away from him. The longer he stayed in Sunset Ridge, the more time he spent with Kylie and Junie, the more he wanted to be a better man and have a future with them.

"Do you want to go by and look at the old bank?" he suggested as they drove into Sunset Ridge. The little town had settled into twilight, and the sun fading over the western horizon turned the trees into dark silhouettes and created a lavender and orange glow over the buildings.

Small towns had their own kind of beauty. Maybe

that was the small-town boy in him talking, but he couldn't think of much that would be prettier or better than riding through this little place with her at his side and the view of the countryside and old buildings.

"The bank?" She looked perplexed. "I've seen it my whole life."

"I know, but I thought we could look at it through the lens of the Valentine's event—what needs to be done or purchased for decorations."

"I guess we could take a peek inside."

He turned onto the street that led to the town square. Her little shop sat in darkness with just the night lights twinkling from inside. Chuck's looked to be packed with cars lined up and down the street and customers coming and going. He turned right and pulled down the street to the bank, a building that had been built in the early 1900s. It had a brick exterior, large plate-glass windows and wide steps leading to the front door.

The Realtor stood out front, waiting for them to arrive.

"Why is she here?" Kylie asked as he parked.

"I asked her to meet us. We can't get the real feel of the place without going inside."

"This seems like a lot of trouble. But I do love going inside and poking around."

"I thought you'd like that."

"Thank you." She hopped out of the truck, and he hurried to catch up.

"Kylie, it's good to see you." The real estate agent held up the key. "Mark said the two of you wanted to take a look at the building. This is such a great place. I've had several people look in the last month."

Of course she would say that. He almost chuckled at the sales pitch. When Kylie gave him a sharp look, he managed to put on a straight face and followed the two women inside.

The building had potential. It had the high ceilings of its generation, polished wood floors, brick walls and large rooms. It also had an upstairs that had been recently used for apartments. That brought his plan together in a way he hadn't expected.

"Is this zoned residential?" he asked.

"It's a commercial property, and yes, the apartments can be rented. It's a multiple family dwelling. Sunset Ridge doesn't have a lot of zoning laws, as you know. They only ask that a commercial building be used as a business and only the upstairs be used for housing."

"Interesting." They walked upstairs, and he wandered through a large, two-bedroom apartment with black cabinets, tall, narrow windows and the same hardwood flooring as the downstairs.

"Why is this interesting?" Kylie asked as they walked into the second apartment, which was smaller than the first, but followed the same design.

"I want a place in Sunset Ridge, for when I'm in town."

He let it go at that and led them out of the apartment and back downstairs. The downstairs happened to be the original reason for their viewing of the property.

"This place has so much potential," Laura the Realtor said as she led them through the open main room. "This room is large enough for most types of gatherings. There are two large restrooms that were installed about ten years ago. Back here, you have a kitchen."

She led them through the building to the kitchen, then to a meeting room, next the promised bathrooms.

"What are you thinking, for Valentine's Day?" he asked Kylie.

"I mean, I never really thought we could do this, but definitely music and dancing."

"I'm thinking white tulle, twinkling lights, kind of a fairy-tale event."

"Really, that's where your mind goes?" Her eyes twinkled with amusement.

"I mean, yeah, really."

"I see," she said with narrowed eyes. "There's something you're not telling me."

"You know me too well. What if I said I want it to be a surprise?"

"I'd be suspicious, but I guess there's no way to force you to tell me."

"Nope."

They asked Laura for a few minutes to wander the building alone. She had a few calls to make, so she stepped away, and they walked back to the kitchen.

"I wanted this building." Kylie ran her hand down the stainless-steel countertop. "I pictured a place where couples could have a romantic dinner on Friday night, or maybe use it for showers and birthday parties."

"What stopped you from buying it?"

"The price. I didn't want to spend all of my money on a building."

"Why didn't you ask?"

She stepped close, facing him. "Because I didn't want anything else from you, Mark."

"What about now?" He needed to do this in the right way, or she'd walk out and never listen to him. "What if I want this building as an investment? I want it because it's a place where I can come and have time with my daughter. I want to spend more time with Junie. She shouldn't feel abandoned by her father, and I need a relationship with her."

"Okay and…"

"I'll buy it and give you a budget for renovations. Turn it into whatever you want. A restaurant, a venue, catering, whatever you can dream up."

"I can dream big, Mark."

He touched her face, tracing his fingers down her cheek. "I want you to have your dream."

He could give her this. Maybe to make amends for the dreams he'd taken, maybe because he wanted to see just what she'd do with her skills. He didn't believe in himself enough to try and be a part of this dream, but he wanted to make it happen for her.

All of his plans overwhelmed her. He'd obviously been thinking about this for a while. Everything would change, but change was a part of life. Nothing ever stayed the same.

She needed a minute to process.

She walked out the back door of the bank to the grassy area that had once been parking. She loved this little courtyard area. She turned around, imagining it as it could be. She imagined the events that could take place here. She hadn't wanted to love this building and this idea of his so much.

"What do you think?" he asked, coming to stand next to her.

"Oh, Mark, I see it. I see this as an outside courtyard, reception area. Tables, walkways, a water feature, twinkling lights."

His shoulder bumped hers. "You didn't want to love the idea. I knew you wouldn't be able to help yourself."

"I do love it." The admission came easier than she would have imagined. "It's a brilliant idea."

"But it needs the right person to oversee the adventure. That person is you."

"You can't buy me."

She felt his shoulder move. He was laughing.

"I mean it," she said a little more firmly.

"I know you do. I'm not trying to buy you. I'm making a sound business decision."

She looked up at him, at his strong jaw, his firm mouth, twinkling gray eyes. She noticed the spot where he'd nicked his jaw while shaving and the scar from a fall when he was eleven. The Rivers boys had been a rough bunch, prone to fighting, but just each other. They'd ridden bulls, ridden broncs and played hard.

"It could work," she admitted.

"But you're not completely sure of doing this with me."

"I'm afraid, and I'm trying to 'fear not.'"

"Let's make a deal." He spoke softly, his fingers touching hers, but he didn't hold her hand. "Talk to me."

"We are talking."

"I mean, tell me what you think and feel. When you're worried, angry, even happy, tell me. If we can talk about it, we can be more intentional in this relationship. Even our friendship needs to be intentional."

He looked so determined, as if this might be the most important moment in their lives. A turning point. Or maybe a new beginning. They'd been children together and teenagers together. They'd set out on a grand adventure, intent on having fun and not thinking beyond the moment. They hadn't worked on becoming better together.

"This mature, grounded you is frightening. I like this person a lot, and I'm afraid he'll leave and not return."

"Believe me, that's my fear, too. I'm doing my best to hold onto this guy."

She felt her lips tug upward, but then seriousness grabbed her again. He was right; they had to talk. "Mark, I'm worried about Junie. I'm worried about my heart because I know that you want to have a place here so you can share our daughter. I feel sick to my stomach at the thought of splitting her up, a weekend with you, a holiday with me, summer vacations torn between the two of us. I'm her mom and…"

He pulled her into his arms and held her tight. She didn't cry, but she leaned in, needing to feel comforted, and he knew how to comfort.

"Shhh, stop worrying. Tearing our daughter apart, pulling her back and forth, that's the last thing I want for her, or for you. I'm not buying this place with that in mind. Yes, I want to spend time with her, but we'll do it in a way that works for all of us and that makes the two of you feel comfortable."

"Thank you." She sniffled and pulled back from his embrace. "Okay, the other fear."

"There's more?" He said it with a brief flash of dimples, but she also saw a look of hurt. She didn't want to hurt him.

That thought surprised her. At one time, she would have liked to hurt him. Now, things had changed; she'd changed. She wanted him to be happy, to be well. For his sake and for Junie.

"There's more. I don't want you to breeze in and out of her life at your convenience, because she loves you and you'll hurt her. She needs to know when you'll be here and when you're spending time with her. Not here for weeks and nothing for months."

Junie had been a toddler when Kylie left Nashville.

She'd barely known her daddy, and she'd adjusted to his being gone. The few times she'd seen him in the following years, she'd liked him, had fun with him, but they hadn't bonded. Now there was a bond. Junie loved her daddy.

"I will also be intentional in my relationship with my daughter."

"You like that word a lot." She studied his face, wondering where all of this intentionality came from.

"I do. I learned it in therapy and might have ignored it, somewhat. But in the past couple of weeks, it really hit home that *intentional* means deliberate. I need to keep that in mind in my relationships, to be deliberate in the time I devote to the two of you and to bettering our relationship."

"This isn't about me," she insisted, knowing he would ignore the statement.

"It is." He brushed a strand of hair from her face, pushing it behind her ear. "Have I told you how much I like this silvery hair of yours?"

"Thank you, but you're changing the subject."

"I am. Just accept that I need to do this, not just for you and Junie, but for myself."

"I can accept that." She pulled at a strand of her silvery lavender hair. "The truth about this. My hair is going gray, and it made me feel old to be gray in my early thirties, so I dyed it the color of gray that I chose."

"It's beautiful, and so are you." He touched his forehead to hers. "I really want to kiss you."

"I'd rather you didn't." The words didn't come easily. "That isn't true. I would actually like it very much, but I know it isn't wise."

"Now that's honesty." He didn't move away. "I guess that means the answer is no?"

What answer did she give to his humor-laced question? She wanted to say yes. She also knew they couldn't blur the lines, not when they were becoming friends again. Grown-up friends.

"The answer is still no. We shouldn't kiss."

"I won't kiss you."

"That's good."

Slowly, he moved away, and she instantly missed his presence. After so many years of being angry, resentful and hurt, somewhere in these past two weeks she'd started to enjoy the journey of friendship. Even stranger to want his touch, to want his lips on hers. She shivered and pulled her coat around herself, feeling a sudden chill.

"We should go in," Mark said, noticing her awkward gesture. "It's getting colder all the time."

"And dark." She glanced at her watch. "Junie will wonder where we've gone."

"She is having fun and not even thinking about how long we've been gone."

Laura found them still standing in the backyard. "What do you think? We could write up an offer if you're interested."

"We want to pray about it," Mark told the agent. He looked at Kylie, and she felt that shiver again. Not the cold, then, but his presence.

She nodded, agreeing with him. In the years they'd been together, they'd never prayed about the decisions they made. They'd rushed through life, taking their chances, making mistakes and laughing when things worked out.

"Oh, of course. So, I'll contact you tomorrow?" Laura looked confused. Kylie felt for her, but she didn't want to back down on praying, on taking their time and getting this right. It wouldn't be her money paying for the building, but she'd have an investment of time and energy.

"Make it Monday," Mark answered decisively. He looked at Kylie, and she nodded. Monday it was. That meant he'd still be here, in Sunset Ridge and in their lives. At least until Monday.

It wasn't his coming and going that worried her, it was his personal decisions. What if he couldn't stay sober? What if he couldn't continue to put them first, to be intentional in this new relationship they were building?

He'd always been her best friend. When their marriage fell apart, she'd missed that friendship. Now that she had it back, she didn't want to lose that part of him again.

Chapter Twelve

Mark stood on the front porch of the house, waiting for Buck so they could head to church. A cat circled his legs, a mangy yellow cat with one ear torn and a scratch on his face.

"You're a mess," Mark said as he reached to pet the cat. A loud meow thanked him for the attention, and the cat purred and rubbed against his pant leg.

"Pet that thing and he'll think he lives here," Buck grumbled as he came out the front door.

"As fat as that cat is, I'm sure someone has already made him feel like this is his home. I'm guessing that someone is you."

"I'm not soft," Buck growled, but he leaned over to pet the cat. "I just kind of like animals that are as worn out and scarred as I am."

"I can see the attraction," Mark observed. "You ready to head to church?"

"Depends on what we're driving. Do we have to take that truck of yours? That thing rides rougher than an old buckboard wagon."

"What do you think we should take?"

"I think the Cadillac since it's Sunday."

"Is that really any better than my truck?"

The Cadillac lived in the detached garage at the back of the house. It had been bought new the year before Izzy left, and it had remained in the garage for most of his childhood and teen years. He and Matthew had snuck it out a time or two, when Buck hadn't been clear-headed enough to realize what they were up to. They'd driven it to the drive-in movies and, once, to Tulsa to see Izzy.

"It's got less than fifty thousand miles on it."

"Because you wouldn't take it out of the garage for a decade or two."

"It's a classic." Buck tossed him the keys. "Take it for a spin, you'll see."

"Oh, I've driven it once or twice."

"How's that?" Buck asked as they raised the garage door and entered the dark confines of the metal structure. "I kept the keys hidden."

"Matthew found them. We took this car out a time or two. The girls loved the Caddy."

"I guess it's too late to ground you." Buck shook his head as he went to the passenger door of the car. "You boys raised yourselves."

They got in, buckled up and, a few minutes later, were cruising toward town. "We did okay, Buck." Mark glanced at his dad. "None of us have been to jail. At least not for any real length of time. We're fairly honest, and we know how to support ourselves."

"I worry about Jonah."

"I know you do. I worry, too, but I know he has to find his own way." The youngest of the Rivers brothers had always been the wildest, most likely to rebel of the group. He rode bulls and lived a hard, dangerous life on the road.

"I'm really sorry for letting you boys down. I wish I'd gotten sober a lot sooner, when it mattered."

"I feel the same way about myself." He pulled into the church parking lot and found a space for the car. "I forgive you."

"I know," Buck said. He patted Mark's shoulder in an awkwardly affectionate gesture. "I guess we make our mistakes and learn by them. I'm praying for you and Kylie."

"Me, too."

Matthew greeted them at the doors of the church. He had a look on his face that immediately set off warning bells.

"Whatever it is, the answer is no." Mark tried to scoot around his brother. He spotted Junie and Kylie and intended to head their way.

"I really need your help." Matthew reached for his arm. "Mark, you know I can't lead the worship."

Mark laughed at the image of his brother trying to lead the singing. "Well, at least that's the truth."

"I'm begging for your help."

"Begging?" He shook his head, hoping to dissuade his brother. "Matthew, there has to be someone in this congregation who can do this better than I could, and someone more qualified."

"No, today you're the one." Matthew put an arm around his shoulder and drew him into the church. "Mark, I want you to do this."

"What am I supposed to sing?"

"Take a look at the old hymnal. You know the songs. We have a guitar. Give it a try."

"For you. I'm only doing this for you."

"Sure, okay." Matthew grinned as he walked away. "Thank you."

As Mark headed down the aisle in the direction of Kylie and Junie, he pulled off his cowboy hat and gave his ex-wife a wink. Her mouth hitched at the corners, and then her eyes widened.

"You cut your hair!" She put a hand to her mouth, and then she laughed a little. "Oh my. You look like fifteen-year-old Mark after Buck took the clippers to you all."

"Thanks, I think. Buck did take the clippers to me last night. This time with permission."

He sat down next to her, and she touched his shorter locks. He'd done it for her because it mattered.

"I love it," she said. "You look like my…"

"Your?"

"Friend. You look like the boy I grew up with."

"I am." He cleared his throat a little. "Matthew asked me to lead worship."

"Go you!" she said cheerfully.

"I'm not qualified."

"Mark, stop doubting yourself. If God leads you to this moment, then He is going to be with you."

"I have to pick the songs," he lamented.

She handed him the hymnal. "You know these, and you know other songs, songs that mean something to you. Pick the music that ministers to you, and I know you'll minister to this church."

He took the book from her hands and spotted several songs that he knew he could do, but then he thought of one that wouldn't be in this book. A song about God being the one who breaks chains and makes a way when there doesn't seem to be a way. He found it on his phone.

When he went forward, he felt a hitch of doubt, but he also felt a heavy dose of God. He wasn't alone as he walked to the front of the church and picked up the guitar that Matthew had left there for him. He smiled at the instrument and then at the congregation.

"When Matthew asked me to do this, I told him I'm not qualified. Then I realized there have been a lot of men before me, much stronger than I am, who also thought they weren't qualified. The Bible is full of men who made mistakes, who doubted themselves, doubted their faith, and then were used by God to do great things. I'm still finding my way. I'm not a Paul or David or a Joseph, but I'm a man who has struggled, who has failed, who has found his way back. I guess most of you remember the last time I sang in this church. It was a Garth song, and it wasn't one of my finer moments."

Laughter greeted that comment, and he smiled. "Hopefully, today I can do a little better."

He started with a few of the standard hymns. When he got to "I Surrender All," he felt the tears stinging his eyes as the words truly hit home. Had he surrendered? He felt in his heart that a surrender had happened. The congregation sang along, but he barely heard their voices. As the song ended, he swiped at the tears that had fallen free. He started the last song, the worship song that wasn't in the book.

The congregation knew the song and joined him. The chains had been broken, and he'd been set free. God had made a way. He sang the chorus twice, and then he set the guitar down and walked off the stage. Matthew met him. The two looked at each other, and then Matthew hugged him tight.

"And you thought you weren't called."

Mark shook his head. "Not now, big brother. Let me have a minute."

Matthew patted his back as Mark walked back to his

family. His wife, his daughter. He sat next to Kylie, and she reached for his hand.

"That was beautiful."

He couldn't speak, so he nodded. She gave his hand a squeeze.

Matthew had stepped to the stage and stood behind the pulpit.

"I'm going to read a few verses," Matthew said. "And then we'll pray and be dismissed. There are moments when God says the work is done. This morning, after that worship service, the work is done. Now is time for prayer. It's time for God to change lives."

Mark felt an overwhelming need to cry. He shook it off.

"What are you going to do with that?" Kylie asked as the service ended and they left the sanctuary together.

"With what?"

"The music, Mark. That worship service was special. What you did up there…" She gave him a serious look. "Do not tell me you didn't notice."

"I noticed how it felt for me, and I hoped others felt it, too."

"You'll pray about it."

He nodded in agreement. What else could he do? He couldn't tell her that he had a career and it had nothing to do with leading a song service at his brother's church. God had opened this door, this once, for him to see that he could lead, but it wasn't his job.

Sometimes God's people are called to make tough choices. The random thought came to him, but he dismissed it. He knew his path.

Kylie let his hand drop, which meant something. Maybe she'd grown tired of him, or disappointed? He could understand that. He'd often been disappointed in himself. He'd often disappointed her.

The church had planned a potluck that day, not merely for the congregation to spend time together, but also for the Valentine's Day planning committee to work on tying up loose ends. In less than two weeks, they would bring together all of their ideas, and hopefully, the night would be a success. Their town desperately needed this to be a success.

"How are you feeling?" Mark asked as they made their way through the food line.

"Better today," she answered. She hadn't thought much about it, but yes, she was definitely feeling better. She'd gotten more sleep the past few nights. The medication the doctor had given her seemed to be making a change in her body.

"You seem surprised," he said.

"Not really, just relieved."

"Relieved?"

She shrugged. "I felt like I should have felt better sooner and I wanted to make sure—my doctor wanted to make sure—the infection was taken care of."

"I wish you would have told me. You matter to me. I want to help if I can."

She had so many things she could say to that. She should have mattered more when they were married. She was no longer his problem, his responsibility. She didn't want to say those things because she didn't want to hurt him or the progress they'd made in their relationship. It felt good to be friends again.

"I agree," she finally said. "I should have said something sooner."

"What can I do?" he asked. "I could take you to a specialist. I know there are decent doctors here, but maybe we should go to the Mayo or somewhere. Isn't that where people go when they need real answers?"

"Mark, I'm fine. The blood tests show that I'm on the mend."

He brushed a hand through his now much shorter hair. "We need to hire someone to help you. And we shouldn't take on the bank if it's going to cause you to be stressed."

"Stop," she told him. "Mark, you have to let me handle this. It's my health, and I'm being proactive."

"I know you are, but I also know that resting is going to be important. The last thing you need is more work. I'll be around for a while, but we need to make sure you have someone to help at the coffee shop."

"Mark, I'll take care of it."

A small, silly part of her had wanted him to stay and help, to be the one who took part of the load. She knew that wouldn't be their relationship. He had his career. Her life was here.

"I know you will. I just want to make it easier for you."

"Everything okay here?" Parker came up behind them. She put an arm around Kylie, but she gave Mark a questioning look.

"I just told him about the tests."

"Ah, I see. He's going into the 'I'm the man and I need to fix this' mode?"

"Something like that." Kylie winked at him, hoping he would relax.

"I think she needs to hire someone at the coffee shop."

"I would agree with that," Parker said. "Even though she is healing and getting stronger, help is always good."

"Traitor." Kylie pushed Mark forward. "Fill your plate."

He did, piling on fried chicken, mashed potatoes, salad, a roll, a pasta dish. She shook her head as she watched him scoop out potato salad.

"Did Ora Sutters make this?" he asked Parker.

"I think so."

"I've always loved her potato salad." He moved on to the desserts.

"He's a mess," Kylie said, more to herself than to Parker.

"I think he's a mess because he loves you and doesn't know what to do to fix the situation."

"Love?" Kylie shook her head. "I'm not even sure what that means. I always loved him and felt pretty sure he loved me."

"Love is a strange, intangible thing." Parker looked at her plate. A salad, roasted chicken and green beans. Parker had always struggled with her weight. "I'm not doing this. I'm having cheesecake."

"Same," Kylie said. "Intangible. That's a good description for love. It isn't the physical thing we feel. Love is putting others first. It's sacrifice. It's caring."

"It's commitment in the worst of times." Parker helped herself to the cheesecake. "The committee is at the back table. They're discussing the bank and the best way to use the building. Matthew said Mark made an appointment with Laura to look at the building."

"He did. It's a fantastic place and has so much potential."

"The two of you looked at it?" Parker said this with a smirk.

"Don't read anything into this. He wants to buy it and let me run it."

"I think you'd make something special of that place."

"Except that now he thinks I'm sick and I'm not."

They joined the ladies and two men who were on the committee for planning the Valentine's Day in Sunset Ridge event. Mark moved so she could sit next to him.

"What are we discussing?" Parker asked as she sat down next to Kylie.

"We're just discussing the way we plan to decorate the square," Mark told them. "The tent will be set up in the center of the lawn. The lights will be strung and music will play. The restaurants have special menus that will be posted. I think they're going to have a punch card. As people go from vendor to vendor and to the stores that are open, they can get the card punched and be entered in a draw to win a gift card package for businesses in town."

"I love that idea," Parker said. "What about advertising?"

Lena spoke up. "I've taken care of that. We have advertising in three area papers. I have fifteen vendors signed up to be in town. If it is too cold, we're going to move them into local businesses. Kylie, would you be willing to let a vendor move into the coffee shop? The nice thing is, heat for the vendor and extra traffic for you. We have to look at this as long term. These are potential customers for years to come."

"I'd gladly give space to a vendor." Kylie smiled at Lena. "As long as it isn't a food vendor. That would make things awkward."

"Oh, definitely. We'll make sure it's a craft or jewelry."

"What about the bank?" Parker asked.

"That's going to be a special surprise," Mark told her. Kylie gave him a look, wondering what he meant. He wouldn't tell her. She could tell by the shuttered look on his face. He had something in mind, and he planned on keeping it secret. At least from her.

"I think this is all coming together quite well," Lena said at the end of the meeting. "Mark has given us great ideas. I'm really looking forward to seeing how the public reacts."

They dispersed. Parker hurried off to find her husband. The others left in search of more food or their families. Kylie pushed to her feet.

"I have to find Junie. She was going to the playground with friends."

"I'm sure she's fine," Mark assured her.

"Mark, what are you going to do in the bank? For Valentine's Day."

"It wouldn't be a surprise if I told you." He gave her a cheeky grin. "I know you're curious, but trust me, this will be fantastic."

"You'll definitely be here? I don't want Junie disappointed."

"I'll be here. Kylie, I wouldn't be anywhere other than here with you and Junie."

What did she say to that?

He leaned in close. "Kylie, we're going to be okay."

"We? You and me, Junie? I don't know what you want."

"I want us." He kissed her quickly, taking her breath in the process.

"No. Us doesn't work," she told him. "We want different things."

"We can work." He seemed so sure. She was anything but sure.

"We're working on being friends," she reminded him.

"And we'll keep working on being friends. In the

meantime, I'm working on being the man God called me to be. The man who cares for his wife to the best of his ability."

"But I'm not your wife."

"I know you're not. If you decide you can't be more than my friend, then I'll be the best friend you need me to be."

"We're in two separate places," she reminded him. "I'll never go back to Nashville. I won't put Junie through that."

"I know." His hand held hers. "I get it. Kylie, I know the statistics for alcoholics. I might struggle. I might fall. The last thing I want is to hurt you."

"Mommy, Daddy, there you are." Junie ran down the hall to greet them. "Are we going to Aunt Parker's for dinner tonight? She said we could."

Saved by the tiny human who loved them both and didn't understand the incredible conflict between them. Kylie pulled away from Mark because she couldn't think with him standing next to her, his hand touching hers.

He answered Junie, telling her they would go to Parker and Matthew's. She wanted to tell him they couldn't. She needed to go home and clean house. She needed to do laundry. She needed to do anything other than spend more time with Mark.

Chapter Thirteen

The cookies were sprawled out in order, each heart frosted in pale pink with darker pink for the words Mark had spelled out. He found a strange sense of accomplishment in each creation. Buck had baked the cookies, but Mark decorated. They weren't too shabby as a team.

He didn't even feel silly, standing in the kitchen of Kylie's coffee shop, an apron around his waist and the chef hat she'd jokingly given him scrunched on top of his now short hair. He glanced at the clock. He'd been here since five in the morning. She should be showing up at any moment.

They'd had this routine for the past week. He showed up early. She arrived with Junie in tow an hour later. She already looked healthier. Their relationship felt healthier.

He found it hard to think about leaving. He couldn't ignore his responsibilities in Nashville forever, but this felt right—this place, his wife and daughter. His phone calls from Nashville, from the new agent, had been insistent that time was of the essence. At the moment, Kylie and Junie had to come first. This time together mattered.

More than anything in life, he wanted to fix what he'd broken. He didn't know what that meant for his career, but he knew the future with Kylie and Junie mattered. No matter how it looked, together or just co-parenting as friends, he had to fix their relationship.

He wanted more than friendship. He wasn't going to lie to her or to himself about that, but he knew that friendship and trust needed to come first.

The ding of the front doorbell alerted him to her arrival. Mark stepped back, wanting his creation to be the first thing she saw as she walked into the kitchen. He smiled, listening to Junie's excited chatter. The kitten had slept with her, and it never missed its litterbox, she informed her mother.

Kylie sounded thrilled.

"Daddy, are you in here?" Junie's sing-song voice called out. Today she wore slippers; he could tell by the shuffle of the soft sole on the tile floor.

"I'm here," he answered. As she came around the corner, he put a finger to his lips to keep her from ruining the surprise. Her eyes widened when she saw the cookies, but she nodded and remained silent.

Kylie was shuffling around in the front, putting away her purse and preparing the coffeemaker. He peeked around the corner, not exactly patient as she fiddled and kept him waiting.

Not that she knew that she was keeping him waiting. Junie grinned up at him.

"Mommy, I think there's a mouse." And then she put her hand to her mouth and whispered, "She hates mice."

"Thank you," he leaned in to whisper. He wanted to hug his daughter and spin her in circles. She was precious and funny, and he'd missed out on knowing her the way he should have known her. He'd let alcohol rob him of her earliest years.

Never again.

His goal was to always put his wife and daughter first. First. Ahead of self, ambition and temptation.

Kylie hurried into the room, obviously worried about a mouse infestation. She looked around, saw him, spotted Junie and then noticed the cookies.

"You've been baking." She approached.

"Actually, Buck has been baking, and I decorated. What do you think?" He wanted her to love the cookies. More than that, he wanted her to love him.

"They're very pretty. Are we serving these for Valentine's Day?"

"That's my plan, but this batch is for you."

That was when she noticed the message on the cookies, and she shook her head at him. Be. My. Valentine. Each cookie had one word, and they were lined up in order. Junie began to clap and giggle.

"Mommy, say yes. Say yes."

He'd left two cookies to the side. A YES cookie and a NO cookie. Like his daughter, he wanted to prod her to pick YES. He didn't know what he'd do if she didn't. He'd never really asked her on a date. All of their lives they'd just been with each other.

Her hand hovered over the wrong cookie. He wanted to push the other in front of her. A slow, sly smile slid onto her face, and she gave him a sideways look. Junie edged in closer, as if she, too, wanted to push the correct cookie into place. The suspense made his heart race as he waited, praying she'd pick YES.

Slowly, her hand moved, and she pushed the YES cookie forward.

"Yes, Mark, I'll be your Valentine." And then she

picked the cookie up and took a bite. "Oh, this is really very good."

"Can I have one?" Junie reached for a cookie.

"Only if you promise to also be my date," Mark told his daughter.

"Daddy, Valentine's Day is for big kids, not little kids."

"But this Valentine's Day is for families," he said as he gave her a hug and then reached to pull Kylie to his side.

Kylie set the remainder of the cookie on the counter. Her smile disappeared, and she became serious again. "We should get to work. Junie, remember that today is history day. You have a project that I'll help you with after you read."

"Okay, Mommy. I love history. We're learning about women who helped during the Revolutionary War. There was a lady who pretended to be crazy so she could take ammunition to soldiers."

"Mad Anne Bailey," Kylie supplied.

"That's the one." Junie skipped away with her bag of books.

Kylie watched their daughter disappear into the little office before she spoke again.

"We have to talk."

He gave a quick nod. "Okay."

"About us."

"Us?"

"I'm serious Mark. This is serious."

He knew it was. He looked at the cookies, the YES cookie now half eaten. Junie had taken the NO cookie. This had been for fun. He'd considered cookie message boxes for the Valentine's Day event.

He told her that and explained. "I thought we could

leave them plain and people could buy them as messag[e] cookies. We could frost the cookies with the message[s] the customers ask for."

"That's a great idea," she conceded. "But us, that'[s] where we're at."

"I know. And I'm being serious. This is about th[e] two of us doing what we should have done fifteen year[s] ago. We should have dated. I should have asked you out rather than assuming we would naturally be together. [I] didn't put effort into our relationship. I took us—too[k] you—for granted."

She brought her gaze up to meet his, and he saw th[e] troubled look in her dark eyes. "How does this end?"

"Or begin? Maybe continue." He liked those word[s] better than "end." "I'm not sure, Kylie. I wish that [I] could say I trust myself completely. I don't, so how can [I] expect you to trust me? I came here determined to see[k] your forgiveness and leave. I stayed, and the longer [I] stay, the more I miss you in my life."

"I think maybe this is a bad idea, Mark. It's goin[g] to give Junie the wrong idea. It's going to make thing[s] more complicated between us. I'm just not sure abou[t] putting Junie in this relationship. She's a little girl wh[o] is learning to adore her daddy, and you could break he[r] heart. My heart can handle it, but I have to protect hers."

"Hurting the two of you is the last thing I want t[o] do."

"Then maybe we should back up a step. Let's no[t] make this a date. We'll be together on Valentine's Day but I'll be working, and you'll be around town helping with the event. At the end of the day, that's probabl[y] the best plan."

"I can respect your decision," he said. His phon[e]

dinged, and he picked it up, read the text and set it back on the counter.

"Important?"

"Nope." Just troubling. "Just work stuff."

"You've neglected your own career to help with mine. I understand that you need to get back to your life."

"I'm committed to this event and to helping you get some rest."

"You don't have to worry about us." She reached for her cookie and popped the last bite into her mouth. After chewing it up, she gave him a cheeky grin. "Those are really good."

"Thank you. I think you just ate your answer."

"I did." she asked as she went to the fridge for a bottle of water.

"So is that your answer for me?" he asked.

She nodded and then gave a pointed look at the office, where Junie watched a TV show, pretending not to listen.

"You came here to make amends and you've done that. I think dating is a complication neither of us need right now."

"You're right," he agreed. The look on his face remained hopeful.

The door chime dinged.

"Customer." Kylie hurried off, leaving him with his thoughts and the messages from his agent.

Several weeks ago, he'd started on this journey, believing it would be simple. He'd been delusional, thinking he could separate himself from what he felt for Kylie, for Junie. He'd planned on protecting them from him. He should have known it wouldn't be as simple as coming to town, making a few apologies and going back to Nashville to his career.

He still didn't completely trust himself, trust tha
he was what they needed. He didn't trust that he coul
keep them safe—from himself.

After the morning rush, Kylie left the front counter i
Mark's care and went to check on Junie and her school
work. She found her daughter in the kitchen, Mark'
phone in her hand. Junie quickly put both hands behin
her back; her mouth tightened, and her eyes grew large

"What are you doing?"

"Nothing," Junie said a little too quickly.

Kylie sighed. "Junie, please tell the truth, not a story
Stories are what we tell that aren't real. They're not th
truth. I want to know what you are really doing, th
true story."

"I peeked at Daddy's text. I heard the sound an
thought he'd want to know that someone sent him
message."

"It isn't your message to read, Junie."

Tears welled up in her daughter's eyes. She scrubbe
at them with her fist, but more fell. The phone droppe
to the floor, and Junie rushed into her arms.

"Daddy's leaving because now people will like hir
again."

"What?" Kylie shook her head, lost in that statement
"That doesn't make sense, Junie."

It wasn't her message, either. She knew that, but sh
couldn't stop herself from asking.

"Junie, what did the message say?"

"It said he's done a good job of fixing things." An
then she cried big tears and buried her face in Kylie'
shoulder.

"Hey, what's up?" He had entered the room, an
he sounded far too cheerful. This moment didn't cal

or happiness. Couldn't he see that their daughter was
upset? His focus went from Junie to the phone on the
floor. "What happened?"

"She read a text," Kylie explained, holding Junie
close.

"Text?" He reached for his phone.

Junie sniffled as she made the accusation. "It said
you've kept your end of the bargain and—I think it was
bargain." She closed her eyes and drew in a breath.
"You cleaned up your image and made up with your
family. Some of the words were big, but I sounded them
out. I'm a good reader."

"Oh, Junie." Mark had the good sense to look sorry.
He covered his eyes with his hands and shook his head.
"That text…"

"It said you're leaving." Junie swiped at her tears.

Kylie wanted to grab her daughter up and hug her
tight. She wanted to run again, to leave behind the pain
this man caused them.

"I know." He shook his head, and Kylie really wanted
him to deny the text, to undo the pain he'd caused them.
"I have to take care of my career. People depend on me."

People depended on him. It couldn't just be them,
she realized. It would always be the band, the agent, the
fans. Kylie moved her daughter in the direction of the
office. "Go watch a cartoon."

"With headphones?" Junie sniffled again, and another tear streaked down her cheek.

"Yes, with headphones."

Kylie watched as Junie did as she asked, and then she
returned to Mark. She couldn't even begin to describe
the anger she felt. She wanted to lash out, to tell him to
leave and to never come back. She wanted to hurt him
the way he'd hurt them.

"It isn't what it seems."

She laughed at that. "Oh please, you always say tha
Usually when you're caught red-handed that's your de
fense. I used to give you the benefit of the doubt, bu
no more. So what was the deal, Mark? Did they te
you they'd take you back if you could use us to polis
up your image?"

"No," he started. "Well, yes. But that isn't why
stayed. It isn't why I've been helping you and spend
ing time with you."

"Of course it isn't."

"I love you." He spoke it so softly, so sincerely. He
heart almost melted, almost gave in.

"No, don't say those words." Her heart couldn't tak
those words. "I can't do this again. I can't take the con
stant fear of the floor falling out from under me."

"I'm coming back," he told her, his voice still calm
still so sincere that she wanted to believe him.

"I'm sure you are." She studied his face, wanting t
see something in his expression, in his eyes, that tol
the truth. "Mark, did you come here knowing abou
this deal? What is it—to make yourself look like a fan
ily man?"

"My agent called me a couple of weeks ago."

"I see, so all of this has been about you, not about u
The intentional living, building our friendship."

"That wasn't part of the deal," he told her. "I cam
here to see you, to ask you to forgive me. I stayed be
cause I wanted to stay. I stayed to help you and to spen
time with you and with my daughter."

"I wish I could trust you. I don't want to go back t
that life. I don't want to go back to never knowing wha
will happen next."

"I'm asking you to trust me."

Trust. The word meant so much, or for him, so little. All of the talk about being intentional. She'd believed him. She'd fallen for every single word because he'd seemed sincere. He still seemed sincere. That made it even more upsetting.

Maybe if he'd told her about the deal, been honest from the start. He hadn't, and that meant everything to her. She didn't need his kind of chaos. She needed a peaceful home, a peaceful life.

"You have to go." She closed her eyes against the tide of emotion that took her breath. "You should tell Junie goodbye. Tell her you'll visit next week, and you'll see her on Valentine's Day."

"Kylie, please…" His voice sounded ravaged, but she didn't care. She felt ravaged, as if he'd wrecked her, wrecked her heart.

She shook her head, unwilling to have a conversation that meant he would try to convince her to change her mind. She'd been down this road too many times to fall for that trick. Apologize, promise to never do it again, smooth sailing for a bit, and then it would come again, and they'd repeat the cycle.

For Junie, she would put an end to the cycle.

Chapter Fourteen

The door chimed. Kylie ignored it. She needed to fin
someone to help in the coffee shop. She'd resisted th
idea for years, but now, having had Mark here to help
she couldn't deny that she needed someone to fill in an
give her time off. If she could find someone she clicke
with, someone who would love her shop and her cus
tomers, she would hire them.

"You look serious." Parker shifted Faith from her lef
side to her right, and then she wrinkled a brow and se
the little girl down. "I am not sure why I keep carryin
you. You have two perfectly adorable feet."

"She'll let you carry her until she's ten." Kylie looke
up from the paper in front of her. "Do you know Dodi
Calder?"

"Not that I know of. Might know the face." Parker hel
her daughter's tiny hand but stepped closer to look at th
filled-out application. "You're hiring someone? I though
you had Mark trained to be your second in command."

"He's gone." Kylie managed a smile and she felt
little bit of pride in the fact that her eyes remained dry
"It's not as if Mark Rivers was going to trade in his lif
for the life of a barista."

"That would be a big change for him, but you never know. Wait and ask when he gets back."

Kylie shook her head. "No, he's going to be in and out, but not permanent. Don't get me wrong, I'm glad that he will be here for Junie. She needs him."

"Wait, something happened?" Parker came around the counter and helped herself to a cup of coffee. "Do you have chicken salad? And cheesecake. I think this looks like a cheesecake moment."

"I've eaten my weight in cheesecake," Kylie admitted. "I'm just done, Parker."

There, she'd said it. She was done. And the feelings that had been growing, the ones she'd thought were genuine, possibly forever, those were gone, just a mirage.

"I kind of thought the two of you were working things out." Leave it to Parker to keep digging.

Kylie closed her eyes briefly, just long enough to get her emotions under control.

"We were working on being friends. He had this thing about being intentional in his relationships. More like intentional in not telling me why he had really come here. I'm so angry and…"

"Hurt."

She slipped a finger under her eye to stop the tears that she'd proudly kept in check but were now threatening to break free. "Yes, I'm hurt. He came here to fix his image. This is why we're not good together, because he does these things. He comes in like the hero, rescues me, makes me love him and then hurts me all over again. Actually, this hurts worse, because I thought that maybe we were fixing our marriage. That's silly, because our marriage ended years ago."

Parker grabbed a tissue from a box on the counter and handed it to her. "Men."

For some reason, that made her giggle. "Yes, men. And this man, I've always loved him. I still love him. I just wanted him to love us just as much."

Parker started to say something, but then seemed to change her mind.

"How's Junie?" she asked.

"Missing him, of course. When I left Mark, she was too young to understand and to realize he was no longer with us. Now, she knows. I've made the best of it. I told her he's coming back and she will have visits with him."

A few more tears trickled down her cheeks.

"What are you going to do?" Parker asked, pouring a second cup of coffee and handing it to Kylie.

"I'm going to keep cleaning my house and organizing drawers, as if that will fix my life. It's such a ridiculous habit."

"It's a coping mechanism."

"That's a nice way to put it." Kylie grabbed a cloth and wiped up the coffee drips. "And there I go again."

"Let me take Junie for the day. She can come out to the house and play with Faith. Faith loves having someone to boss around."

At the mention of her name, the toddler gave a toothy grin. She was perfect, the sweetest with her round cheeks, bright eyes and curly dark hair.

The door opened, and Laura the real estate agent stepped in, her business smile firmly in place.

"Kylie, it's good to see you." Laura approached the counter, where she placed her leather briefcase.

"I'm sorry, didn't Mark tell you he's leaving the state?" Kylie asked. She'd forgotten about the bank, about the dream, about sharing that moment with Mark as they'd planned what all could be done with the building.

"Oh, he called me. Actually, we met last week." She

pulled papers out of the briefcase and pretended to look for a clean spot on the counter, which was spotless. "I don't want these to get wet."

Kylie forced a smile. The last thing she wanted to do was deal with Mark's business. Parker put a hand on her arm and stepped forward, moving her to the side.

"Maybe this should wait for Mark's return. I think his plan is to return Thursday morning. We can have him call you."

Laura slid a pair of reading glasses into place, and she looked over the top, giving Parker a hard stare. "And you are?"

"Mrs. Matthew Rivers. Mark is my brother-in-law. Whatever dealings you have with him would probably be best done in person with Mark."

"I'm not here to see Mr. Rivers." Laura pulled off the glasses, and her business persona melted away. She offered Kylie a real smile. "Kylie, I'm here to see you."

She pushed the papers across the counter. "Mr. Rivers purchased the bank. He arranged it all before he left. The building is yours."

"No." The word came out on a sob. She couldn't focus as tears ran down her cheeks. "Why does he have to do things like this?"

"Because he's Mark. He's a little wild, a little bit chaotic, but he wanted you to have that building." Parker gave her a side hug, holding her tight for a few seconds.

"It's too much. I can't take that building. I don't have the ability to manage both."

"Maybe move this business to the bank?"

"I love my little coffee shop."

Professional Laura returned, sliding the glasses back in place. "I don't know what you'll do with it, but it's yours. If you could sign this document for me?"

The agent handed her a pen. Kylie's hand trembled as she put her signature on the line. Another useless tear streaked down her cheek, this one from being humbled by this gesture.

"A few more signatures and we'll be finished." Laura moved through the papers, explaining what each meant and why it had to be signed, acting like she didn't see the tears. "I'm sorry this is so much, but there are serious legal ramifications if I don't explain and if you don't sign."

"I understand," Kylie said, feeling a little lost in this process and a myriad of emotions, both good and not so good.

Laura put some of the papers back in a folder and handed over a manilla envelope with the most important ones.

"There you go, Kylie. The building is yours. I can't wait to see what you do with it."

"Thank you."

"You're welcome, but the one you should be thanking is Mark. And before I go, could I get a latte and one of those cupcakes?"

"Of course." Kylie grabbed a cup and made the drink, not spilling a drop, even with hands that continued to shake. She handed it to the Realtor and pointed to the stand with sugars and creamers. "You can add whatever you'd like. I'll get your cupcake."

"Smells wonderful. Thank you."

A few minutes later, Laura left with a little wave and a "catch you later."

"Wow." Parker shook her head and then said it again. "Just wow."

"He bought the bank." Kylie stared down at the documents in her hands. "I can't stop crying. Why does he have to do such kind things? Or is this another way to make amends? Will I always question his motives?" The questions rolled out.

"I think in time, if he proves himself, you'll trust him or question him less. The bank building is a grand gesture."

"It is."

"What will you do with it?" Parker asked.

"Laura showed us the place. It's fantastic with high ceilings, big windows and beautiful wood floors. There are apartments upstairs. Oh, and outside, a perfect area for a courtyard. I think it would make a lovely venue."

"Do you have the keys? I want to see inside!"

"Oh, I hadn't thought about that. I own it!" She dumped the envelope Laura had handed her, and the keys fell onto the counter. "I can't do this. It feels like strings."

"Maybe you should talk to him and ask him why," Parker said in her very logical way.

"Talk." Kylie closed her eyes and breathed deeply, feeling the calm that came. "We had discussed that, the need for communication, for being more intentional in our conversations rather than letting misunderstandings grow."

Parker gave a little chuckle as she lifted her daughter, snuggling her close. "Mark is becoming his brother."

"Maybe he read Matthew's book?"

"Highly possible," Parker said. "Talk to him. Don't make rash decisions or judgements without knowing his intentions."

"I'll talk to him. I just have to work up the energy and the strength."

"Good. And I'll take Junie. Do you care if she spends the night with us?"

"That would be great. I need to go see my mom."

"How is she doing?" Parker asked after blowing raspberries on Faith's pudgy little hands.

"She's angry, and it's my fault. I imprisoned her in a horrible, abusive detention center."

"Nice place, huh?"

"It's a beautiful place. They have lovely grounds, a fountain, the food is decent. But in her mind, I had her locked in jail."

"You know you're going to have to find a way to listen to her without taking it to heart, which is easy for me to say, and I'm sure hard to do."

"I know. It's just tough because I already feel guilty for putting her there. She simply can't be left on her own, unsupervised."

"No, she can't. You're doing the right thing."

"It doesn't feel that way. And then I feel bad because I don't want to visit her."

"Also understandable. Give yourself a break, maybe don't go see her tonight. Instead, go home and take a bubble bath, play with the kitten, take a walk."

"I could use a night off," Kylie admitted. "I need to breathe, to pray and to figure out what I need to do next. Mark is going to want time with his daughter. She needs time with him."

"It's going to be a change for you all."

"It is, and I have to tell him to stop buying things. He is paying for my mom's new facility. He said that's one less thing I have to worry about. Now he's bought the bank for me. I am angry with him, and I want him to just let me have a little time to process these feelings, but he keeps doing all of these kind things that really touch my heart."

He'd said he wanted her to trust him. If only he hadn't hidden his real reason for being in Sunset Ridge. To her heart, that had been a deal-breaker.

* * *

Mark left the meeting with his agent and the record label executives feeling freer than he'd ever felt, except maybe when he left the treatment facility last spring. That had been a good day. A day of second chances. Today had been a day of big changes and unexpected decisions.

He guessed, in a sense, this day had brought second chances as well.

He decided to walk for a bit, just to clear his head and adjust to the decisions he'd made. The weather had turned pretty, nearly seventy degrees. For a February in Nashville, that was a bonus day, the kind of weather a person looked forward to all winter. He decided to take a walk downtown. It had been a while.

He passed old haunts and a few new places that he hadn't been to, places that had opened since he got sober. These days, he avoided those places because they were a temptation. He avoided old friends, too. He'd let them all know that it wasn't anything personal, just a choice he'd had to make.

The sounds and smells were familiar, though. Country music, some good and some bad, the occasional argument, the smell of booze and fried foods. He drew in a breath and smiled. The smells of home. He hesitated outside a place he used to love. He'd started singing in that dive bar. He'd been "discovered" in that bar. The owner had pushed for him, showcased him whenever possible and told everyone who would listen that he'd found a star.

He should go inside and say hello to Bub. He started to. He took a step, and then he hesitated. Bub just happened to peek out the door and saw him standing there.

"Well, I'll be. If it isn't Mark Rivers. Son, I haven't seen you in nearly two years."

"I've been keeping a low profile." That was an understatement if ever there had been one, but they both knew the truth.

"I'd invite you in, but that might not be..."

"Bub, I'd love to be able to come in, but I'm going to give you a hug and move on down the road."

They stepped close and gave a good, solid man-hug and then they stood there on the sidewalk with familiarity and past friendship between them.

"So tell me what you're doing down here. Are you back to work?" Bub asked, his gray hair thinning and his middle a little more paunchy than it had been all of those years ago.

"I came here to meet with the label and my agent. I did meet with them."

"Well good for you. You're sober and getting back to work."

"I'm not," Mark said, needing to say it out loud to someone. "It's hard to say it, but I think there are more important things in my life than music."

Far more important. So important he didn't know how to breathe without them. He missed them, his wife and daughter. And if he had a chance to make things right, that's what he wanted, more than anything.

Bub gave him a long and almost fatherly look. "Son, you've got the right of it. You lost yourself, but it appears you are on the right track. As much as I like to pat myself on the back for discovering new talent, I also want the best for you personally. Maybe music isn't it."

"Maybe it isn't." Just saying the words brought a lightness he hadn't expected. He grinned at the bar owners. "I think I'm on my way."

They both laughed, because he'd said that when Bub introduced him to his first agent. Now the way was a different direction, but one that he thought would lead to more joy. Real joy, not the artificial, made up of stuff, kind of joy. "I'm definitely on my way," he said again, a little easier.

"That you are," Bub repeated from that day so long ago.

"Thanks for everything, Bub. I'll be back around to see you."

"You take care of yourself," Bub told him with a slap on the back.

"That's what I'm trying to do. See you soon, my friend."

"I hope so."

As he said it, he realized he wasn't sure. Maybe this would be his last day in Nashville. The first day in a future that looked, or felt, more promising. As if maybe he'd overcome a dark place in his past and he could trust himself to be the person that Kylie and Junie deserved, the person they could trust.

He walked on, but this time, he headed back to the parking lot where he'd left his car. After tossing his phone on the passenger seat, he picked it up and opened his camera roll. The images picked him up. Junie had taken a few selfies without him knowing. He'd never delete those photos. As a matter of fact, he planned on getting them printed and framing them. Photos of his daughter doing homework, but taking the occasional photo of her feet, her face, her work. And there were pictures of Kylie. Junie had snapped pictures without her mother knowing. Kylie at work. Kylie smiling at a customer. Those picture filled his heart.

Right there, that was his reason for being, for making the decisions he'd made, for working hard to earn money that would provide a living. Man, he missed them.

He missed them, and now they were the reason for walking away from the career that had provided the living that had moved them out of poverty.

He hit a button on his steering wheel. "Call Jake."

He hadn't talked to Jake in a month. He shouldn't have neglected the relationship.

"Hey, big Mark, how you doing, buddy?" Jake, always up, always cheerful.

"I'm in town," Mark told his friend. "Would you mind getting together?"

"Anything for you." Jake hesitated. "You okay?"

"I will be. I just need a minute."

"You going to your place?" Jake asked.

His place. The house he'd lived in with his wife and daughter. It wasn't his place; it was Kylie's. There were rooms where he thought he could still smell her perfume. There were still diapers on the shelf in the nursery. The house held so many memories, so much of their lives together.

"Yeah, I'm going to my place." He hadn't slept there in months. He'd stayed in hotels. He'd stayed with friends.

"I'll meet you there," Jake said.

Jake actually beat him to the house. Mark had stopped at the store.

Mark eased through the gate and up the driveway of the brick French country–style home that had been their dream. Not too big, Kylie had insisted when they purchased the place. She didn't want to hire someone to clean or to help with the baby. She wanted a home that they could grow into, fill up with children, invite friends and family to visit.

Today it felt hollow, more hollow than when he'd come home after rehab. More hollow than the day she'd left. Their footsteps echoed. As he led Jake through the house, he realized it was time to put the place on the market. He didn't need this house, not here, in Nashville.

He smiled at the thought of the loft above the bank. Laura had delivered the papers to Kylie. He wondered how she'd taken the surprise. Had she been excited or angry? Maybe a little of both. He grinned, imagining her put out by his taking such a step without telling her.

"How was Oklahoma?" Jake asked as he watched Mark put away the groceries he'd picked up on his way to the house.

"Dry and flat." He laughed at the description. "Actually good, and not flat, not in the northeast where I live."

Mark pulled eggs out of a bag, along with milk and butter.

"What are you doing?" Jake asked.

Mark looked at the ingredients. He hadn't really thought about it, but now he knew.

"Making cupcakes. In rehab, they told me to find a new hobby, and I wasn't sure what that would be, until I started baking. Funny story, my dad also bakes."

"Funny," Jake said with a hint of sarcasm.

"Maybe not funny," Mark said. "Ironic."

"You struggling?" Jake asked as he cut to the chase.

"A little." He started with the eggs, then melted butter, added the milk and sugar. Vanilla. He couldn't forget vanilla. "I messed up and didn't tell her about the conditions of my new contract."

"Better public image, right?" Jake had taken a seat on a barstool. "I'm guessing that didn't go over too well."

"It definitely didn't go over. We were building a relationship, working on trust. I had this grand scheme that if I could be intentional in my relationships, and although we're no longer married, if I could love her the way Christ loves the church, maybe we could be us again."

Us, but better, he thought. More grounded. More mature.

"But you didn't tell her the most important piece of the puzzle."

"Right." He turned on the beaters and let them do their work on the batter. "I'm an idiot."

"It happens to the best of us. Trust is fragile, you know that. She trusted you with her teenage heart, with your daughter and then…"

"No need to remind me. I messed up. I know that, and I won't begrudge her the anger she feels for me. I thought we could be friends." He pulled out the cupcake pan and used cupcake liners before filling each with the vanilla batter.

"That smells pretty good, and it isn't even in the oven yet."

"I have skills."

"And talent." Jake leaned back in the seat. "Do you have coffee?"

"I do. I can even make you a latte if you'd like."

"I'll stick with plain old coffee." Jake scratched his cheek. "Oh, I remember, the ex-wife opened a coffee shop and bakery."

"Yes, she did." Mark set a timer on the oven. "And I've been helping her. She had an appendectomy. Happened my first night in town."

"That must have been rough."

"Stop sounding like my therapist. You're a basketball player."

They both laughed. "You are correct. I'm also your sponsor, so it makes sense that I want to get a feel for what's going on in your life."

"I broke her heart, and she told me to leave."

"I'm assuming you don't have anything in this house that will ruin over a year of sobriety?"

Mark put his hands on the marble counters and stood there for a moment, finding peace, praying for strength. After a few minutes, he opened a cabinet door. Jake joined him, pulling out the bottle he'd kept. Now he realized he didn't want the bottle.

He watched as Jake poured it down the sink. "I told you, don't keep stuff in the house."

"I know. At least I didn't open it. Jake, how long have you been sober? Like continuously, without relapse."

"Relapsed once, four years ago. It was a week that I truly regret. I've been sober for four years." He tossed the bottles in the trash. "The first year is the hardest. You've made it through that year, Mark. Every day you stay sober, your odds of defeating this monster grow."

"I want my family back, but right now, she thinks I was using her to get my career back."

"Country folks do love a little romance and a happy ending," Jake added, unhelpfully.

"This isn't a country song, it's my life. It's my family." Mark stepped away from the cabinets, from the smell of the alcohol. "When I walked away from that meeting a couple of hours ago, I wondered if I'd made the right decision. I even wondered if I'd get a few miles down the road and change my mind. I made the right decision."

"I guess the one you need to be talking to next is Kylie."

"I'll be going back for Valentine's Day. I hope she'll talk to me. I need to introduce her to the new me."

"I don't envy you. Being a single guy, I've never had to worry about hurting a family, just my team and my mom."

"Wouldn't it be nice if life had road maps?"

At that, Jake laughed and tossed his pocket Bible on the counter. "In case you've lost yours."

Mark touched the Bible, then he raised his gaze to meet that of his friend. "Thank you for coming over today."

"That's what I'm for, to be here and be strong for you when you can't. Someday, you can be that person for someone else."

"I also like to call you a friend," Mark said as he palmed the Bible, one of many that Jake always had in a pocket, just in case someone needed it. "I have one of these."

"That's okay, keep that one. I have good notes in there."

Mark thumbed through the text and found the notes. One of his favorite verses was circled. "Resist the devil and he will flee." Resist. Don't give in. Don't fall for the temptations.

He flipped to the front cover, knowing the verse that would be there. Psalm 34:14. "'Depart from evil, and do good; seek peace, and pursue it.' Is it that easy?"

"It doesn't say it's easy. It's just a path forward. You know what you're supposed to do, Mark."

"I do," Mark admitted. "The last thing I'd ever ask Kylie is that she give up her new life, a life that makes her happy."

Her life made her happy. His life without them left him empty and alone. That pointed to only one right choice. He glanced back at the words, to see and pursue peace. He knew in Whom to seek for peace. He also knew the direction the giver of peace was taking him. Home.

Chapter Fifteen

On Valentine's Day, Mark parked his truck several blocks from the square. Jael had joined him. Buck had decided he didn't need to be "traipsing all over town in the cold. Valentine's Day is for the young." They weren't used to spending time together, so the ride had been quiet, with Jael looking out the window and Mark thinking about this night and all the reasons it mattered.

It mattered because, for better or worse, he'd put their Nashville house on the market. For better or worse, he'd told his agent he was positive he wouldn't be signing a new contract. Some things were more important than having his name in lights. Kylie and Junie were more important.

He and Jael exited his truck and started the walk toward the square, still cloaked in uncomfortable silence.

"You know you can't just waltz into this town and pretend you didn't break your wife's heart, your daughter's heart."

"I understand that." The idea that he'd broken their hearts broke his, undid him in a way that nothing else ever had.

As they walked the few blocks to the square, Mark

had to agree with Buck; it was cold. His sister didn't seem to mind a bit. Youth, he thought, and then he chuckled because he sounded like Buck. It felt good, to laugh a little.

"What are you laughing about?" she asked, pushing her knit cap up just a bit and giving him a censuring look.

"I was laughing at myself. I'm thirty-three, almost thirty-four, and I just realized that I've started saying things our dad would say. Like you're not aware of the cold because you're young. When did I become Buck Rivers?"

"When you crawled in that bottle and didn't climb back out for ten years of your life. Did you ever stop to think that you missed out on memories that you can't get back?"

"Thanks, I needed something to drag me down just as I started to feel optimistic."

At that, it was her turn to laugh. "You're welcome. Negativity is my gift."

"You should work on that." He found he meant it. He wanted his little sister to find some joy. Everything about her was serious. "Find what gives you joy."

"I'll take your advice into consideration." She gave a little shrug. "So, back to you, because my life isn't that interesting. What's your big plan tonight?"

"Big plan?"

"I mean, there is one or you wouldn't have arranged so many little surprises for this night without telling Kylie. Obviously, you couldn't hide the details, like the carriages or the princess ball. That's pretty touching, by the way."

"This event is for the community, and it shouldn't be just for the ones who can afford dinner out or the vendors. It will be a beautiful night for families who otherwise can't do something like this."

"All in the name of love and convincing Kylie to give you a second chance."

"Cynical." He bumped his shoulder against hers. "It's for the children. That is separate from my relationship with Kylie. Did you know that there are several stories about Saint Valentine? One is that he was martyred for ministering to persecuted Christians."

"You're not persecuted."

"Yeah, that was a sidenote that has nothing to do with anything. I just wanted to teach you something today, other than to mind your own business. I thought you'd only planned to stay a few days?"

"I needed a break from work and Dad seems to enjoy having me here."

He guessed there was more to the story, but it wasn't his story, and he wasn't going to push for details she didn't want to give.

"I think Buck would like it if you moved in permanently. I'm sure he does get lonely. You can be his farm hand."

"I can't see that happening." She took several steps and then stopped, looking up at him. "I really do hope you fix things with your family. Junie deserves to grow up knowing you're there and she can depend on you."

The statement gave him a glimpse into her brokenness. She'd had more, but maybe she'd had less. In time, he hoped they could talk about what caused the dark shadows in her eyes.

While they'd talked, they'd reached the square. Although the actual event didn't start for thirty minutes, people were already milling about, perusing the vendors who had chosen to set up in the outdoors with tents and small heaters. He appreciated their fortitude, but he would have picked one of the heated buildings that had been offered.

The entire square had been transformed into a Valentine's Day winter wonderland.

The tent, a large white fixture, lit inside and out with Christmas lights, was situated at the far end of the lawn. There were tables set up inside and there would be dancing for adults who didn't want to participate in the princess ball held inside the bank. He could hear the band, a local country group, tuning their instruments and doing sound checks.

Chuck and Jenni Stringer had spiffed up their café, putting white tablecloths on the tables, adding bouquets of flowers and piped-in piano music. Chuck had changed out of the George Strait T-shirt that he typically wore on Saturday nights, and Brody had decided to wear a suit because that was what he'd seen in movies.

Mark glanced in the direction of Kylie's. She'd hired a young woman to help in the coffee shop. The new hire meant that Kylie and their daughter could enjoy the festivities, at least for a bit.

His phone dinged, and he pulled it from his pocket to read the text and then hit reply.

"Who was that?" his nosey sister asked.

"Matthew, letting me know that Kylie and Junie are in a carriage. If you don't mind waiting for me, I'll be back."

"Are you going to hijack their carriage?"

He grinned, winking at his sister. "Something like that."

"I like you a lot better than I used to. Are you going to also drag her back to Nashville? You know she hates the city, right?"

He did know that. "I'm not dragging her back, I'm hoping she'll listen to what I have to say. Say a prayer."

"I'll leave that to you."

His little sister was a broken person. He'd never noticed before. Of course, they hadn't spent much time together. As kids, they'd had the occasional visits, but as adults, they'd rarely crossed paths. He really needed to work on being better for her, too.

But right at this moment, he had a carriage to catch. He hurried down the street, finding it hard to jog in boots. He should have worn his running shoes. Two blocks from the square, he spotted them. The carriage was a pretty white affair, pulled by a couple of deep red Missouri mules. He liked the contrast between the carriage with its pretty lights and the plodding mules who would tire less quickly than most horses.

The driver came to a stop, and Mark hopped in, drawing a shriek from Kylie and a "Daddy, you're back!" from Junie as she leapt into his lap.

"Surprise," he said to his ex-wife and his daughter. "I hope you're enjoying the carriage." He hugged Junie tight as he sat down next to Kylie.

Personally, he'd never seen the romance of a carriage. It was rough, jolting and not really very comfortable. For some reason, people thought it romantic to take a ride around the block in one. He doubted the settlers who traveled across the country in wagons thought they were too romantic.

"I love the carriage," Junie said as she snuggled between her parents. "Did you know they have princess dresses at the church and silly costumes for boys?"

"And here I thought I'd jumped into the carriage of real princesses. I didn't realize it was just a costume."

"Daddy," she said with a roll of her eyes. "You're being silly."

"I am silly, but I do think you are both princesses."

"Mommy is the queen," Junie told him.

Mommy still hadn't spoken.

"Happy Valentine's Day, Kylie." He said it softly, hoping to break down the walls she'd put up. He'd messed up. He'd more than messed up.

"I'm glad you could make it," she said, her gaze dropping to Junie in a pointed way. No conversations with little ones aboard. He got it.

He desperately wanted to tell her everything. He wanted her advice. He wanted her for a partner again. He prayed, had been praying, for healing for their marriage, for her heart.

The carriage took them around the block and then to the square. They drove past Chuck's, and Kylie commented on the crowd inside. There were also quite a few customers in her coffee shop.

"I should…" she started.

"Later," he said. "I'll help you. Parker and your new assistant can handle this for a bit."

Her head craned in the direction of her business, and she exhaled, letting go. Her hand reached for Junie's. The carriage circled to the side of the square where the bank stood like a centurion of the past, guarding its corner with elegance. Lights illuminated the facade and sparkled from inside.

"Thank you for this building," she said as the carriage came to a halt. "I mean that."

"It's going to be something special." He believed that wholeheartedly.

"Let's go in." Junie had lost her struggle with patience.

Mark didn't blame her; it all looked very enchanting. Princesses, princes, court jesters and parents were entering through the double doors that were being opened by doormen he'd hired to give it all a very exclusive feel. Inside, he'd hired a caterer from the city to serve appetizers and desserts. A trio played instrumental music.

He helped first his daughter and then Kylie from the carriage. Her hand slipped into his. He hesitated, wanting to look his fill before handing her down to the sidewalk. Her gorgeous hair had been pulled up in a pretty style that framed her face. Her eyes were wide, her lips parted slightly. She smelled of tropical islands and summer gardens. The top she wore was a deep red and hung past her waist, flowing and silky over black leggings.

Her hand trembled in his, and he held it a little tighter, drawing her down from the carriage so she stood next to him.

"Mark," she started.

He winked. "Call me Prince Charming."

"You've always been charming," she said in a dry tone.

"May I?" He gave her the crook of his right arm. With his left hand, he took hold of Junie. Together, the three walked through the doors of the bank into a room that had been transformed into a ballroom.

"This is…" Kylie gave him an astonished look. "You did all of this?"

"I've never taken Junie to a father and daughter dance. I thought about it and thought there might be other parents who wanted this special moment with their children. Ta-da, welcome to the first annual Sunset Ridge Prince and Princess Ball. Happy Valentine's Day to you both."

Kylie didn't speak, but her dark eyes were luminous with unshed tears. "Mark, sometimes you steal my breath."

He wanted to steal her heart.

He bowed before his daughter, holding her hand as he did. "Princess Junie, could I have this dance?"

She curtsied and then giggled. "Yes, you may. And then you have to dance with Mommy because she's the queen."

"Gladly."

He led his daughter in a slow dance with Kylie just at the edge of his vision, watching. He had so much to say to her. Their future depended on this night.

Kylie watched as Junie and Mark circled the dance floor, talking and laughing. Days ago, she'd been so angry with him. Tonight, she wanted to stay angry, just to protect her heart. She also wanted to hug him for his thoughtfulness, not just to Junie, but to all of the families who were being gifted such a wonderful experience. It wasn't about the money he'd spent, it was about his kindness in thinking of others.

This man who arranged such wonderful things was the man she'd loved, the man she'd married and had a daughter with. She'd taken vows with him to love him forever. She'd taken vows that spoke of love that had no end, that didn't faint and fall apart in a crisis, that didn't give up. She hadn't given up. He had. He'd given up on them.

That was her greatest hurt. He hadn't put his wife and daughter first. He'd put his own wants and needs ahead of his family.

Tonight, she didn't want to think on those things, on the past. She wanted to let go of that burden and live a life free from those hurts. She'd become an expert at letting go. She'd been letting go her entire life. Letting go of dreams, of the hope she'd have a happy home, even in childhood, wanting her mom to be like other moms. She was done with letting go.

She'd always been a determined person. Determined to have better and be better. With or without Mark, she would continue to reach for better.

Mark circled back around with Junie, and the music ended. He bowed again, and their daughter did another excellent curtsy. This time, he bowed in front of Kylie. He extended his hand, an invitation to dance. Kylie closed her eyes briefly, thinking of ways to reject the offer. And then she nodded and took his hand, allowing him to lead her onto the dance floor.

The band began to play a Norah Jones song. Surprisingly, the violinist sang, and she did it well. The sweet words of "Come Away with Me" filled the lofty building, echoing sweetly.

"Did you ask for this song?" Kylie asked as Mark pulled her close.

He nodded, pulling her closer.

They danced well together. In their young and broke days in Nashville, they'd taken ballroom dance classes. They'd tripped over their feet, laughed until they cried, and then they'd found their rhythm and learned to dance.

"I've always loved her voice," Kylie said as she drew close, allowing him to lead her in the waltz.

"I've always loved you."

"Mark, please don't do this. Not right now."

"I have to," he said. She wished he wouldn't. The night was perfect. It was beautiful.

"Can we finish the dance?" she asked.

"We can." They circled the dance floor in each other's

arms. On the sideline, Jael had found Junie and was keeping her entertained.

Kylie watched as his sister led his daughter to the buffet and they began to fill their plates. She didn't have to worry about Junie. She relaxed into the rhythm of the dance.

In that moment, in Mark's arms, Kylie felt whole. She felt loved. She felt all the things she'd longed for from him and none of the things that hurt. As the song ended, he led her away, away from the crowds and their daughter.

They went out the back door, and she gasped. There were candles everywhere, and as they left the bank behind, floating lanterns began to fill the sky. He'd planned this. She didn't even have to ask. Somehow, someway, he'd planned this.

Her heart wavered, wanting to be his. Her brain said to back away, to keep the boundaries that were necessary for safety.

"Why?" she asked, needing answers. They couldn't go back. She didn't know how to go forward.

"Because you're the most amazing person I know, and this night is for you, for you to feel cherished and loved."

Love? She shook her head at the word.

"Kylie, I messed up." He must have seen her roll her eyes. "Okay, a lot. I've messed up so many times. The young me was a stupid fool who got caught up in his own imagined self-importance. Kylie, before I came here last month, it was mentioned that a healthy relationship with my family would fix my public image. But that is not why I came. When Junie saw the text, and you didn't even hesitate to believe the worst in me, I didn't feel a need to try and explain."

"We keep going back to the issue of honesty and communicating," she said.

"Yes, we do. I wasn't joking when I told you I want to be more intentional in our relationship. Kylie, I asked my brother what the Scripture means when it tells a husband to love his wife the way Jesus loves the church. I've spent weeks journaling and praying about this. I'm to treat you as if you're the most important person in my life. I'm to care for you, to uplift you, to sacrifice for you, and I am to put your needs ahead of my own. Our marriage was broken, our family broken, because I put what I wanted ahead of what my family needed. I came back to Sunset Ridge to seek your forgiveness, and then I planned to go on my way because I don't want to put you through that again. I don't want to let you down."

"I think we both have trust issues, Mark."

"I know we do. Neither of us trust me." He said it with that smile of his that touched her heart. "I have come to realize that I was keeping God out of the equation. I, on my own, am a mess of a man. But I'm seeking the man God wants me to be. And that man is your husband. That man is the person who loves you more than he loves himself. He loves his daughter. He loves you more than a career."

"More than a career?" she couldn't help but tease.

"I met with the record label, fully intending to sign the contract. I went back to the house and prayed, and then I put that house on the market, and I called and told my agent that I'd be coming back to Sunset Ridge."

"Okay, you came back. Now what? Do you go back to Nashville to sign the contract?" She felt her heart beat hard against her ribs. She wanted him to give an answer that told her they mattered. She feared he wouldn't.

"I put our house on the market, Kylie. I hope you're

okay with that. I hired a moving company to pack everything and bring it here to storage, so you can decide what to keep."

"You haven't answered my question." And it was starting to hurt, to make her feel afraid.

"I'm not going back to Nashville. I told them there will be no contract, no new album. I had to come back to Sunset Ridge. I left something important here. I left the most important part of me. I left you."

She felt the walls around her heart crumbling. A sudden wave of hope washed over her, hope that this Mark, the man standing before her, was the one that God had brought into her life, and the hope that he was seeking God in a way that would change their lives.

"Did you find it?" she asked. He looked a little confused. "What you left behind."

"I hope so. What I left behind was my wife and daughter. I want you back, Kylie. I want to be the man you can count on, the man who will keep you close and cherish you."

"I'm afraid," she admitted. She drew in a breath, held onto resolve that was quickly slipping away. "I can't rush into this Mark. There is so much at stake—not just our relationship, but Junie, her heart, her feelings."

"I know and I understand. I know you don't want to rush things and you shouldn't. I just want to know if there is a chance that you might love me and give us the opportunity to begin again."

"I do love you. That doesn't take away the fear."

"I get that. I have a whole lot of baggage, but I've given that baggage to God, and I'm going to be relying on Him to help me live each day for Him and for my family. For whatever He calls me to. I want to spend time growing in my walk with Him. I want to prove to you and to myself that I can be the man you deserve, that you can trust."

"Mark, is there a question in all of this?"

He pulled her close and kissed her, keeping her near, drawing her heart to his. He ended the kiss, but he remained close, his forehead touching hers.

"There is a question, but I'm afraid to ask, because I'm afraid you'll say no."

"I'm not going to say no," she said, surprising herself. "I'm also not going to say yes."

He pulled back a step and she saw the glimmer of gold and diamonds in the box he held in his hand. He chuckled nervously. "Now I'm not sure what to say."

"Promise me that you're going to be honest with me and that we're going to continue to work on being the couple, the family we were meant to be. It isn't going to happen in a month. It might not happen in a year, but in time, when we are ready."

"I can make that promise. This is a new ring for a new beginning. It's a promise for our future. That future is in your hands, if you'll take it."

Kylie held out her hand and he placed the ring on her finger. He held her hand for a moment and then he kissed her palm.

"Once upon a time, I put a ring on this finger and I didn't keep the promises I made to you. That ring was purchased by a younger, dumber version of myself, a man who didn't know how to be a husband and a father. I hope that I've grown and learned from my mistakes. I can't promise I'll be perfect, but I promise to be my very best self for you, for our daughter and even for myself."

She closed her eyes, holding those words tight and praying for them both, for their family and their future.

"I'm going to give us a chance, Mark. I want a better version of us, too."

Fireworks rocketed through the night sky, and a lone violinist joined them to play a song about a marriage renewed, two people broken but finding a way to put the pieces back together.

As lanterns floated away on the night sky and cold air touched her cheeks, she felt the warmth of Mark's lips on hers and hope filled up the dark and empty places.

Epilogue

Kylie looked in the mirror, again, worrying that her dress was too much for such a simple ceremony. Jael settled the veil on her head and smiled from behind her, their gazes meeting in the mirror.

"Why are you worrying?" Jael asked. Mark's little sister had become a friend of sorts, even though she still kept mostly to herself and kept her secrets.

"I'm not worrying, not about Mark, not about our relationship." For the past six months, he'd worked hard in the community, helping his brother in ministry, leading worship in church, being the father Junie had needed and deserved. He went to weekly meetings to maintain his sobriety. They talked, no, they communicated. Each night after Junie went to bed, they discussed their day, what was good and what went wrong, if anything. They shared their worries and their joys. They prayed together.

He put them first. At night, after their prayers, he went back to his loft apartment above the bank. After today, he would move back in with his family. He'd courted her for six months. It had been the dating period they'd skipped as teens.

"What is it?" Parker asked as she came forward with the bouquet of lilies and baby's breath.

"I'm walking down the aisle like it's my first wedding, and it isn't. I'm thirty-three, and Mark and I were already married. This all seems a bit silly."

"You were married, but you didn't have a real wedding." Jael stated the obvious. "You got married at the courthouse in Nashville."

"Yes, we did."

"Today, you're going to get married in your home church. You'll have a beautiful reception in the bank to celebrate the occasion." Parker gave her a big smile. The bank had been turned into a lovely venue.

"Yes, it's going to be beautiful." Kylie smiled at the two women who would be her sisters. "I'm so glad you're both my family."

Jael gave her a quick hug. Parker's hug held a little longer.

"Mommy, you're beautiful." Junie slipped into the room. She wore a pretty pink dress, and her hair was curled in ringlets thanks to her aunt Jael.

"You're a princess," Kylie told her daughter. "We should hurry. Let's get this over with."

Parker shook her head. "No, let's enjoy this moment. Celebrate it. Make it a beautiful memory."

"Yes, celebrate. Memories. Blah, blah, blah." Kylie reached for her bouquet. "Is he out there?" she asked Junie.

"He's at the front of the church, and he's sweating bullets." Junie gave a strong nod, her lips pursed.

"Sweating bullets. You've been eavesdropping again." Kylie leaned to give her daughter a kiss on the cheek. "Let's put him out of his misery."

"That's what he said." Junie giggled.

Buck waited for her, and he led her out the door of the church and to the front door of the sanctuary. The double doors were open. Her groomsmen, Matthew and Luke, were waiting. They walked down the aisle with Parker and Jael. Junie came next, tossing silk flower petals as she walked.

Buck held tight to Kylie's arm, and he leaned a little closer.

"I'm real glad to see you all working this out. God planned the two of you. I never doubted that. It's just that things went a little off course."

"We're back on course," Kylie agreed. "Thank you for walking me down the aisle. It means so much."

"You mean a lot to me. I'm glad you gave that son of mine a second chance."

"Same."

As they walked, the song played that the two of them had claimed as their own. The lyrics to "Broken Together" filled the church. A song of being broken and being made whole again.

Broken together.

Mark reached for her hand as his dad nodded and walked away. She wanted to kiss him, to tell him how much she wanted them to always be this way, together. Whole.

Matthew cleared his throat and told them to let go of each other's hands until he gave them permission to take each other by the hand. Mark didn't let go. Matthew didn't argue. Instead, he spoke the words that would make them man and wife, make them a family. And then he told Mark he could kiss his bride.

Mark pulled her close. His eyes were intense; the look on his face brought a shiver down her spine.

"This time, Kylie, it's forever. I will cherish you,

sacrifice for you, make you the most important thing I have on this earth. Trust me."

"I do trust you." God had made it possible to trust, to be healed of their past. "And I love you. I've always loved you."

They kissed and the crowd that had gathered, the people who loved them and supported them, cheered. As they left the church, Brody hurried forward to sing the song they'd given him to sing. "Fly Me to the Moon."

Brody, it turned out, had a very decent singing voice.

* * * * *

*If you enjoyed this Sunset Ridge book,
pick up the previous book in
Brenda Minton's miniseries:*

Reunited by the Baby

Available now from Love Inspired!

Dear Reader,

Thank you so much for taking this journey with me to Sunset Ridge. As you read the story of Kylie and Mark Rivers, I hope that you'll feel the love they have for each other. My hope is that you'll laugh with them and maybe cry a little as they work to resolve the pain of their past.

There are so many young couples who struggle to find the path to a strong and lasting marriage. It's my greatest hope that in this book of just such a couple, others will find hope and a way to build their relationship. Marriage isn't easy. My advice to my married children and to other young couples is this: Do you remember that childhood slumber party with your best friends? You went for one night and decided that two nights would make it more fun, but then you ended up tired of each other, angry and ready to go home. Make your partner your best friend and be willing to talk and work it out because marriage is a slumber party that lasts a lifetime. There will be times that you're crazy in love and times you wish they'd pick up their own dirty socks. Find joy in your life together and be intentional in building your relationship.

Brenda

COMING NEXT MONTH FROM
Love Inspired

UNEXPECTED AMISH PROTECTORS
Amish of Prince Edward Island • by Jo Ann Brown

Amish bachelor Lucas Kuepfer wants nothing to do with Aveline Lampel—until they rescue a kidnapped *Englisch* child. Now Lucas and Aveline are hounded by reporters and discovering they have more in common than anyone suspected. But will their preconceptions keep them from being a perfect match?

THE AMISH BEEKEEPER'S DILEMMA
by Patrice Lewis

After being jilted, Rebecca Hilty moved to Montana to start over as a beekeeper and dreams of inheriting her boss's farm. The only thing standing in her way is cranky farmer Jacob Graber. But when faced with an impossible inheritance requirement, will Rebecca marry Jacob...or lose the farm for good?

A MOMMY FOR EASTER
by Linda Goodnight

Twelve years ago, Rachel and Jake's marriage ended in heartache. Now he's returned to Rosemary Ridge a widower with an adorable daughter. But when old feelings resurface between them, Rachel and Jake find themselves caught between their painful past...and the hope of a future together just in time for Easter.

UNITED BY THE TWINS
Wyoming Legacies • by Jill Kemerer

Reagan Mayer's inherited the perfect building for her new small-town shop. There's just one problem: rancher Marc Young wants it, too. But when he's suddenly charged with caring for his twin nieces, their dispute is put on pause and Reagan volunteers to help. Will caring for two babies open their hearts to love?

THE COWBOY'S SECRET PAST
Lazy M Ranch • by Tina Radcliffe

When the Morgan family patriarch is injured, nurse Hope Burke arrives at the Lazy M Ranch to help him—and see if Trevor Morgan really *is* the father of her orphaned nephew. But falling for a guarded cowboy with a rocky past might be more than she bargained for...

RECAPTURING HER HEART
Sage Creek • by Jennifer Slattery

After losing her job, single mom Harper Moore returns to her hometown with one goal in mind—leaving again. But first she needs money, even if that means working for her ex-boyfriend, CJ Jenkins. Now the sparks are back and it could mean a second chance...if CJ can give Harper a reason to stay.

LOOK FOR THESE AND OTHER LOVE INSPIRED BOOKS WHEREVER BOOKS ARE SOLD, INCLUDING MOST BOOKSTORES, SUPERMARKETS DISCOUNT STORES AND DRUGSTORES.

Get 3 FREE REWARDS!

We'll send you 2 FREE Books <u>plus</u> a FREE Mystery Gift.

Both the **Love Inspired®** and **Love Inspired®** Suspense series feature compelling novels filled with inspirational romance, faith, forgiveness and hope.

YES! Please send me 2 FREE novels from the Love Inspired or Love Inspired Suspense series and my FREE gift (gift is worth about $10 retail). After receiving them, if I don't wish to receive any more books, I can return the shipping statement marked "cancel." If I don't cancel, I will receive 6 brand-new Love Inspired Larger-Print books or Love Inspired Suspense Larger-Print books every month and be billed just $6.49 each in the U.S. or $6.74 each in Canada. That is a savings of at least 16% off the cover price. It's quite a bargain! Shipping and handling is just 50¢ per book in the U.S. and $1.25 per book in Canada.* I understand that accepting the 2 free books and gift places me under no obligation to buy anything. I can always return a shipment and cancel at any time by calling the number below. The free books and gift are mine to keep no matter what I decide.

Choose one: ☐ **Love Inspired**   ☐ **Love Inspired**   ☐ **Or Try Both!**
                  Larger-Print   **Suspense**   (122/322 & 107/307
                  (122/322 BPA GRPA)   **Larger-Print**   BPA GRRP)
                                              (107/307 BPA GRPA)

Name (please print)

Address   Apt. #

City   State/Province   Zip/Postal Code

Email: Please check this box ☐ if you would like to receive newsletters and promotional emails from Harlequin Enterprises ULC and its affiliates. You can unsubscribe anytime.

Mail to the **Harlequin Reader Service:**
IN U.S.A.: P.O. Box 1341, Buffalo, NY 14240-8531
IN CANADA: P.O. Box 603, Fort Erie, Ontario L2A 5X3

Want to try 2 free books from another series! Call 1-800-873-8635 or visit www.ReaderService.com.